Sleigh Bells & Sleuthing

A Christmas Cozy Mystery

B I Skinner

Contents

Chapter 1

"Howieeeeee!" the VFW bar patrons chorus as soon as I tug on the creaky bar door, followed by a rousing cheer of "Scoobyyy!" for my steadfast companion, a caramel-colored, long-haired dachshund I adopted from the local shelter after the love of my life passed away three years ago.

Scooby replies with an excited bark while the corners of my mouth lift in what could almost be considered a smile. One could argue that Scooby likes people more than I do. Don't get me wrong, I appreciate my dear friends, but must they always make such a fuss? I'm here nearly every evening at the Veteran's Hearth Bar on the Pearl Street Mall. For heavens sake, they just saw me yesterday.

This might sound odd, but visiting the bar calls up fond childhood memories of riding bikes with friends after school, especially in the fall, hearing the colorful leaves crunching under our tires, and inhaling the delightful scent of crackling home fires in the hearth. Just as the sun gradually dipped below the horizon and the neighborhood lights came on, my mom would call us in for dinner.

After storing my bike in the garage, the mouthwatering scent of mom's cooking always greeted me in the doorway. My favorite was chili and cornbread night. Mom ladled the piping hot chili into our bowls next to a side of golden cornbread with butter melting in the crevices.

We gathered around the table, chattering on about our day, but even when I was arguing with my siblings and worried about the homework, the important part was being home. That's what it's like when I walk into the bar. The bar is old and a bit tired, just like me, but it's comfortable. It's home.

Memorabilia from various military eras, including photographs, medals, and patches, adorn the walls. It's an environment rich in history and stories. And it's Christmas, so as usual, Sammy, the owner, bartender, and my best friend (next to my dog, of course), has draped twinkling lights, sparkling tinsel, and sleigh bells on everything.

I plunk down in the same worn, wooden chair at the same worn, wooden table I do every time I'm here while Sammy brings me my usual drink—a whiskey sour with a cherry. Don't *at* me. I like those little cherries.

Scooby jumps into the chair next to me, patiently waiting while I remove his red puffer coat. Then he high-fives

Sammy for the treat Sammy always has hidden in a pocket for him.

The coat is a gift from my granddaughter. I assured her dogs don't need coats and Scooby would be embarrassed to wear the ridiculous thing. Naturally, Scooby betrayed me by loving it.

"He's so close to the ground," she pointed out. "He needs something extra to keep him warm." She also suggested boots, but that's where Scooby and I draw the line. After a fair amount of wrestling to get the boots on, he promptly fell over on his side, his little feet flailing.

"Is all this," I ask, gesturing to the holiday decorations, "really necessary?"

"You ask me that every year, old friend, and my answer is the same as always. Yes." Sammy smiles, his twinkling eyes laughing at me. He's wearing what he always wears. An aged leather bomber jacket and gold Army veteran ball cap. His short-cropped silver hair and beard speckled with gray are the only things that indicate he's some years past middle-aged.

"Have a bell!" he says, pulling a sleigh bell from his pocket. It's tied with a bright red ribbon and a tag that reads, *Veteran's Hearth Bar - Where Valor Meets Fellowship.*

"What is this?" I ask.

"It's a bit of Christmas cheer, you grouch."

"I'll be glad when the holidays are over," I grumble. "I nearly got run down by a pack of elderly ladies just now. Everyone rushing about like mad elves, drowning in shopping bags, lost in the commercial Christmas craziness. What is this world coming to?"

"You say that now, Howie, but I see you. I see the work you put into making the kids smile," Sammy points out, a soft seriousness glossing his tone. "Your heart might be hidden behind those grumbles, but it's as big as Santa's."

I brush off the compliment, ignoring the warmth spreading through my chest. I hardly think my heart is as big as Santa's, but I do enjoy overseeing the Pedals of Promise event every year. The kids Sammy is referring to are underprivileged children from the community and children with deployed parents. We solicit donations year-round to provide bikes for them, in addition to hosting a huge Christmas party at the Starlight Community Center.

Kids get bikes, and parents enjoy a festive meal with all the trimmings, along with a ton of other goodies that local businesses donate. The joy it brings to their innocent faces and the laughter that fills the air gives me precious hope for humanity. I cherish it dearly. Just don't tell anyone. I wouldn't want them to think I'm going soft in my retirement. I witnessed more devastation than a person should, serving in the Army and later as a detective in Boulder, Colorado. The fact I can do something for others now, soothes my soul.

"Hey, Jack! What's up?" I shake the hand of another friend who rolls up to the table, where I always keep a spot cleared for him. I'd argue he's too young to be hanging out with all us old fogeys, but he's a decorated war veteran, and I know from experience it's good for him to spend time with those who can empathize with everything he's been through.

During the week, he's an Intellectual Property lawyer for a prestigious law firm in Boulder, and on weekends, he competes in a highly competitive wheelchair basketball league. They're really good. He's been to nationals and everything.

"Thank you!" I tell Bonnie, the waitress when she hands me my usual Monday night dinner. My granddaughter Ellie nags me to eat more vegetables, but I like to point out that there's a piece of lettuce and a slice of tomato on my cheeseburger. Also, potatoes are vegetables. Even if they're fried in oil, they're still vegetables.

The subtle warmth of the whiskey sour, the juiciness of my cheeseburger, the crisp golden fries, and the cheerful chatter surrounding me have me feeling so comfortable I'd almost admit I'm in a good mood.

But, as is often the case, unfortunately, my good mood flips on its head when the door slams open followed by a gust of frigid air, and none other than Ebenita Scroogina darkening the doorway. The bar turns quiet and grim while the bitter cold follows Ebenita right to my table. This should be good. What will she complain about now?

"The Pedals of Promise event," she starts, her voice as sharp and cold as the icicles hanging outside from the roof, "is canceled."

Chapter 2

Ebenita's frigid presence snuffs out any hint of warm fuzzy feelings I was experiencing only a moment ago. Frosty pint glasses halt mid-air with all eyes on Ebenita Scroogina, the thorn in this town's side for as long as I can remember.

I swear she's a dead ringer for the mean lady from The Wizard of Oz. You know, the one who tried to steal Toto. Which makes her the worst person ever in my book.

"You're joking," I snarl at her when I know deep down she isn't because she's Ebenita.

"Do I *ever* joke?" she snaps.

"Then you're lying."

"I have the signed decree right here," she gloats, flourishing it proudly.

She stands tall before me, reveling in her negative power, letting it whirl throughout the room while everyone looks on, horrified, waiting to see what happens next.

I pull my reading glasses from my coat pocket while Scooby and Ebenita exchange dirty looks. After reading it, I hand it over to Jack with the tiniest sliver of hope that somehow it's fake or won't hold up, but I can tell from his expression that it's legit.

He reads aloud. "The City Council of Boulder, Colorado, through a vote of 5-4, hereby rescinds the Pedals of Promise Event Permit for Christmas Day based on increasing concerns over the undue burden the event places on residents within walking distance of the Starlight Community Center. Due to a lack of parking at the Center, the surrounding neighbors must bear the brunt of the traffic increase..."

After that, I tune him out. What kind of person gets a children's Christmas event canceled? And how did she convince 5 council members to do it?

Like the queen of ice she is, she wears a malicious smirk like a cruel ornament to her victory. Silently, she whirls on her heel and heads for the door, making a dramatic exit, the tails of her coat following her like a dark wave crashing into the sea.

The moment the door slams shut, protests erupt throughout the bar. It's a chorus of dismay and disbelief followed by the inevitable storm of anguish, frustration, and bitterness.

Sammy stomps to our table, demanding we hand over the letter. "That witch!" he shouts while Scooby barks in agreement. "I've had it. I've absolutely stinkin' had it. I hope she gets run over by Santa's reindeer on her way home!" he bellows, waving the letter over his head. "She'll regret this, and I'll make sure of it if it's the last thing I do."

While I understand Sammy's rage - I'm feeling it myself - I don't think it's the best look for him to announce it for everyone in the bar to hear.

"I know, I know." I attempt to soothe him. "But it's important we stay calm so we can think of a solution."

"Can we hold it someplace else?" an elderly gentleman sitting near the door asks.

"Where?" Bonnie, the waitress, responds. "It's a week before Christmas. Everybody else has been booked for months."

"There's no way we'll find another venue," a man at the table next to ours chimes in.

"And she knew it too." Jack grimaces.

"Of course she did!" Sammy continues shouting. "She complains about this event and threatens to get it canceled every year. She finally made good on it."

Jack leans in to whisper, "Don't the bikes have to be out of the warehouse on Christmas Day?"

I nod. Last month, they sold the warehouse, where the bikes are stored, to make room for new condos. The new owner graciously agreed to let us keep the bikes there until Christmas, but they must be out before the 26th, when the contractors come to demolish the warehouse. They were adamant about the date. No exceptions. This means even if we wanted to postpone the event, we'd have nowhere to keep the bikes.

"Can we appeal our case with the City Council?" asks a woman sitting at the bar.

Jack shakes his head. "They've all left for Christmas vacation by now. There's a reason Ebenita timed this the way she did."

Once again, the bar erupts in anger. Its fury coils around the room like a gathering storm. Sammy, his eyes burning with indignation, leads the charge. I've never seen him so angry. Ebenita has been tormenting us for years, but this was the final straw for him.

Threats to harm Ebenita fly fast and furious. Most of them are just hot air. At least, I hope so, but people really need to calm down.

The tension dissipates a little after Jack announces a round of beers on him, promising everyone we'll figure something out. After a while, most finish their beer and head out, insisting we keep them updated while offering to help in any way they can.

I worry because Sammy is still livid.

The inevitable round of phone calls I'll be making, will have to wait until tomorrow, and at this point, I've done everything I can. Plus, Scooby is getting antsy, and I doubt Sammy would appreciate him lifting his leg on a bar stool.

"I guess it's time for Scooby and me to head home," I tell Jack.

"I'll keep an eye on our friend over there," he says, nodding in Sammy's direction.

"Please do. Let me know if you need anything. Maybe I'll come up with a solution walking home."

Jack smiles, but only faintly. We both know it will take far more than a short walk to solve this mess.

After I pay for my dinner and bundle Scooby into his coat, we head out into the cold winter night, my heart heavy with worry about what might happen to the needy children on Christmas.

The sky, now a mystic blend of twilight hues, provides the perfect backdrop for delicate snowflakes floating from the heavens. Their intricate wonder adorns the town in a soft, glittering blanket. But I appreciate none of it. Not with the weight of dozens of distraught children pressing down on me. How can I tell them there will be no bicycles or festive Christmas dinner?

The Veteran's Hearth bar is located on the Pearl Street Mall, a walking mall nestled in the heart of Boulder and conveniently within walking distance of my house. As we trudge home, shoppers scurry past us, oblivious to our troubles. Their joyful laughter and cheerful greetings barely register with me.

I'm blind to the shop windows fashioned to look like pages from a storybook, full of Christmas warmth, velvety red stockings, gleaming ornaments, and carefully crafted holiday delights. I'm deaf to the gentle hum of classic Christmas carols flowing through the air as well.

I've decided The Grinch had it right. The beginning part, anyway. Where he just stayed home with his dachshund and complained about the holidays. Not the part at the end where he makes everybody happy because that's not happening this year. Nope. This year, the mean Grinch won. Even Scooby senses the gravity of the situation as we make our way home. His usual bouncy steps are gone, his ears no longer bobbing while he walks.

Once we leave the mall area and enter the residential portion on 9th Street, we pass sturdy brick houses - their windows aglow with tender flames of fireplaces and twinkling Christmas lights. Sturdy trees line the streets dressed in festive attire - strings of soft, glowing lights intertwining with the naked branches, creating a pathway of luminous lace. I actually thought it was all so pretty only a few hours ago. Now, it's meaningless.

I'm so distracted by Ebenita's malicious stunt I'm surprised when I discover we're already home. I climb the steps to the porch of my Tudor-style house, where Scooby and I are happy. As happy as I can be, anyway. Three years ago, my wife Lisa was diagnosed with pancreatic cancer, and within months she was gone.

At least once a month, my daughter Olivia insists I move to Florida to be near them. Forget that. Have you seen the giant snakes living there? With my granddaughter Ellie attending the University of Colorado, I tell everyone I have to stay to keep an eye on her. That excuse will hold for a couple of years, at least.

But as I unlock the door, I nearly stumble on a small shiny package with a note: *Hi Gramps! I made you some rum cake. Hope your day went well!* My evening was a catastrophe until now, anyway. My granddaughter's surprise gift instantly cheers me.

The house is dark except for the porchlight and a small tabletop lamp in the front window. I don't decorate for Christmas. That was my wife's thing. She loved the holidays. I don't hate them; but I don't enjoy them like I did when Lisa was alive.

As I kneel to remove Scooby's coat, the threats people made in the bar still ring in my ears. As much as I'd love to knock Ebenita down a peg or twelve, I sincerely hope no one makes good on their promise. It would only make things far worse than they are right now.

Chapter 3

My morning always starts the same way, with Scooby eagerly licking my face until I grudgingly abandon the warm cocoon of my bed. Then, I make coffee while he goes outside to do his business.

But after a night filled with tossing and turning, I finally came upon a solution. At least, I hope so. I'll swallow my pride and go to Ebenita's house to reason with her. Perhaps I can make some kind of deal where I guarantee no one will park in front of her house. I'll stand guard in person and shoo people away if I have to. I know somehow the city council will have to make an exception, but it's the only solution I can think of. Whatever it takes.

We have 30 children expecting new bikes for Christmas, more than 30 families eagerly counting on a holiday meal they may not get otherwise, and a more than patient property owner expecting to arrive at an empty warehouse on December 26th to start the new construction. I refuse to let any of them down.

Imagine being a child whose parent (or, in Timmy Tempkins case, *both* parents) is deployed and will miss Christmas this year. Or imagine being the child of a single parent working two jobs who can barely afford Christmas dinner, much less presents, expecting a bike for Christmas, only to be told it can't happen because a mean lady doesn't like people parking in front of her house once a year.

Truthfully, it's more than just free bikes and food. It's a huge party where the community gathers to break bread and celebrate the season. Sammy plays Santa Claus, restaurants donate food, and volunteers pass out presents. Most of the volunteers are grizzled old vets like me who don't have families to come home to, so it's meaningful for us, too.

In the worst-case scenario, we could ask the families to pick up their bikes at the warehouse, but what about dinner? What about the party? Then it's nothing more than haphazardly passing out bikes to those who are able to visit the warehouse.

There's no community experience and no meal. Some of these families are counting on the big holiday dinner they couldn't afford otherwise. In addition, the restaurants have already ordered extra food they plan to prepare on Christmas Day. Will it go to waste now? How will we ever get them to agree to donate again if this year's event is canceled unexpectedly? How could Ebenita do this? I'm so angry I can practically feel my blood boil over.

After coffee and breakfast, I dress in my retirement uniform (as my granddaughter calls it): a plaid shirt and corduroy pants. My graying hair is cut short and always neatly combed, of course—a decades-long habit forged by military life.

Scooby and I stay in shape by taking daily walks around Boulder. *Scooby's* doctor said we need to be careful with his long back, so no getting chubby allowed. *My* doctor said *I* need to stay in shape to keep my blood pressure and cholesterol in check —so, no chubby for me either, unfortunately.

"Scooby, let's go!" I tell him. His nails click on the wood floor as he runs to the door; so excited about an early walk. I bundle him in his jacket before stepping outside. The first breath of cold air is invigorating, filling my lungs with the pure essence of winter.

A pristine blanket of new snow covers the landscape, untouched and undisturbed, glittering under the pale light of the early sun like a million tiny diamonds. Each step is a soft crunch, the snow compressing under my boots, leaving a trail of footprints in our wake. The usual sounds of daily hustle - cars, footsteps, distant conversations - are conspicuously absent, replaced by the whispers of a gentle breeze rustling through barren branches.

Ebenita lives a block from the community center and her house appears to frown upon the seasonal cheer with its bare, undecorated façade. Yikes. Maybe I should hang up some Christmas lights at my own house. This is so dreary. The *KEEP OFF LAWN* sign only adds to the grinch-like atmosphere.

I rap firmly on her door, clearing my throat and running through my speech in my head. But silence is my only greeter - no Ebenita. I ring the bell this time, but the chimes echo hollowly across the threshold. No footsteps, no voices, not even a rustling noise from within—just the cold, uninviting panels of the door staring back at me, along with a *No Soliciting* sign, of course.

I sigh in resignation. I worried she wouldn't be home or might refuse to answer the door. But I'm prepared for this. I already wrote a note letting her know I'd like to make peace and figure out a way to keep the community event on and the cars away from her house. I slide it under the door, hoping against hope for a Christmas miracle.

Scooby nudges my hand with his pointy nose, making a huffing noise as if he's acknowledging our fruitless visit and is urging us on. As we retrace our steps, he occasionally pauses to acquaint himself with the various scents the snow trapped overnight.

Despite the snow and cold, as usual, it's a beautiful sunny day in Colorado, so we choose to take the longer route home, passing by the Starlight Community Center. But as we approach it, Scooby, with a sudden and unexpected fervor, darts across the center's empty playground and around the corner to the north side of the building.

"Scooby, you get back here!" I shout at him. What has gotten into that dog? He never runs off willy-nilly. He always sticks close to me. I give chase, only to find him staring at a scraggly, leafless bush, barking frantically. "Scooby, what's wrong?" I hope he hasn't cornered a squirrel or some helpless cottontail rabbit. But then I see them. A pair of legs sticking out from underneath the bush. Uh oh.

I move in closer, taking care not to disturb anything. I may be a *retired* detective, but the old instincts kick in once I suspect Scooby has discovered a body. First, I have to make sure it isn't a homeless person or a drunk college student who has passed out in the snow. If that's the case, they'll need immediate medical attention. I can only hope they haven't been here all night.

However, as I move closer, my hopes for a reasonably happy ending are squashed.

It's a body all right.

Now I know why Ebenita didn't answer the door.

She's dead.

Chapter 4

My experienced eyes rapidly assess the grim scene: her body is sprawled awkwardly, with a whisper light coat of snow providing a macabre cover, and the surrounding snow a resting place for the harsh reality of death. From what I can tell, without getting too close, she was strangled.

Upon discovering that, my breath catches in my throat, my heart pounding heavily against my chest like a rapid drumbeat. Years of experience have steeled me against the brutality of crime scenes, yet this one strikes an unusual chord of somber reality with the outspoken threats from last night once again ringing in my ears.

My eyes narrow to a pinpoint focus as I instinctively analyze the scene, the detective in me awakening to the call of duty amidst the shock. The fresh snow adds a layer of difficulty to determine what happened, but there's no drag marks, and I don't recall seeing any near her home.

I curse myself for not paying more attention to the scene surrounding her place, but how could I have known at the time I'd find her body just a block away? For all I knew, she was at the grocery store. Or refusing to answer the door because she didn't want to talk to me.

The winter-bare bush doesn't appear broken or damaged, so she didn't fall into it. Nearby, numerous jumbled footprints stagger like a puzzle, so there was at least a brief struggle. But even with a light coating of fresh snow, some of the footprints are clear.

A man could easily overcome her. It would be more difficult, although not impossible, for a woman to strangle her, so I won't rule that out for now. There are two sets of footprints but they're scattered so it's difficult to tell them apart. One clearly matches Ebenita's small boots and the other has an unusual tread pattern.

I dig my phone out of my pocket and slip off my gloves while my fingers quickly grow numb in the cold. My thumbs move clumsily over my smartphone, a device I have a love-hate relationship with. My granddaughter taught me how to use it, and I admit, it comes in handy. I snap several pictures of the crime scene to study later. No, I'm not getting involved with the case. Just a few simple pictures because my memory isn't what it used to be.

A glint in the snow near her outstretched hand sparkles. I kneel to get a closer look. My heart sinks when I recognize a shiny sleigh bell with a ribbon and tag attached. I pull a pen from my pocket to flip the tag even though I already know what it says. *Veteran's Hearth Bar - Where Valor Meets Fellowship.*

I remind myself that anybody could have dropped this, but deep down, I realize how bad this looks. After examining everything I can, without compromising the crime scene or getting myself into trouble, I dial 911.

"Yes, this is Detec--, I mean, my name is Howard O'Sullivan, and I've just found the body of Ebenita Scroogina in some bushes on the north side of the Starlight Community Center."

"Sir, are you sure it's real?" the operator asks.

"Of course it's real! Why would I call 911 if it wasn't?"

"I apologize, sir; it's just that we often get calls from people who swear they discovered a body when it's only college kids playing a prank with a CPR dummy or a large bag of trash."

"I assure you, this is a body. This person was alive last night, and now she's deceased."

"You know the victim?"

"Yes."

"And you saw her last night?"

"Yes."

"Where and what time did you see her?" the operator presses.

"Could you just send a squad car?" I'm annoyed she's giving me the third degree. I was a detective long enough; I know where this is going.

"Sir, we've dispatched a car, and they're on their way. Please don't touch anything."

"I promise you I won't," I respond grumpily before hanging up, cutting her off in the middle of her request to stay on the line. I feel a twinge of guilt for my abruptness, but I don't have time for her standard operating procedure.

Within minutes, a black and white, along with an unmarked car, roll up to the scene, their lights flashing but no sirens. The community center, a beacon of town spirit, is now a crime scene. I still can't get the threats out of my head. Could I have prevented this?

My mind races as I give my statement to the officer, where each word I say creates more questions than answers. He's a young man who I'm convinced isn't even old enough to buy beer. These days, everyone looks way too young. I desperately want to ask his age, but I hold my tongue. I remember when I started with the force, and the older guys teased *me* for looking so young. It hits me like a ton of bricks when I realize I'm now one of *them*.

"How did you find her?" the officer asks, his breath forming clouds in the cold air.

"My dog," I nod at Scooby, now shivering in my arms, which I suspect is more from nerves with all the excitement, than the cold. "He led me to her."

"And this bell?" the officer holds up an evidence bag containing the sleigh bell, now a piece of silent testimony.

"It was lying next to her when I got here. But I don't know if it was already there, or if *she* had it, or if it was the perpetrator."

It bothers me that I'm worried about that darn bell. Could someone from the bar last night have done this? A lot of people made a lot of threats, and not just last night. The entire town has despised Ebenita for years.

"I'll need your contact information, sir, for follow-up questions."

"We have his contact information, Officer Hart," Detective Laura Rodriguez says, approaching us.

"Uh, we do?"

"This is retired Detective Howard O'Sullivan."

"Oh! Uh. I'm so sorry. I didn't know."

"Don't worry about it, son," I tell him.

"Detective." I nod at her.

She smiles graciously. "You can take the detective out of the job, but you can't take the job out of the detective?"

"Something like that." I chuckle.

I've dealt with Detective Rodriguez a few times. I don't know how old she is either, but I'd guess around mid-30s. Her long dark hair is tied back in a ponytail, and she's wearing dark gray wool pants with shoes unsuitable for snow. I'm sure she hadn't planned to be at a crime scene like this today. It's usually quiet around the holidays. We'd anticipate the standard drunken arguments at parties, but not murder.

Only now do I notice a crowd gathering, a mix of early shoppers from the mall and nearby residents drawn in, no doubt by the flashing lights and commotion as additional law enforcement arrives on the scene. I can already imagine the rumors spreading as everyone's eyes focus on the three of us huddled together.

My thoughts tumble like snowflakes in a storm. I intended to mend fences with Ebenita, to understand her, to appeal to a sense of community I hoped lurked beneath her frosty exterior. Instead, I find her in the one state beyond the reach of diplomacy or reason.

"Your dog is adorable. Is it okay if I pet him?" Detective Rodriguez asks.

"Sure."

As she slowly lifts her hand for Scooby to sniff, his tail thumps madly against my side, and he licks her. Scooby has a thing for the ladies. Young, old, and every age in between.

"What's his name?"

"Scooby."

She giggles. "Appropriate. They tell me Scooby found the body."

"He did." I know she wants me to say more. She asks a simple question, then waits for me to fill in answers to questions she *didn't* ask. I did it all the time when I was on the job. People are uncomfortable with silence, so if given enough leeway, they'll answer way more than the police ask.

"You're definitely a retired detective, aren't you?" She smiles.

"That I am." I nod crisply.

"Okay, I'll get right to the point. Are you normally out in this area so early in the morning?"

"Scooby and I walk around Boulder every day. I don't live that far from here, you know."

"I heard what happened at the bar last night," she adds.

"What bar is that?"

"The bar where one of my officers was waiting for a date when Ebenita dropped a bomb on all of you."

"It sounds like you already have the answers you're looking for," I tell her a little more bitingly than I'd like.

"No need to get testy with me, Detective. I only want the truth here."

I know what you're thinking. I haven't told her I just came from Ebenita's house or that I left a note for her. She'll figure it out eventually. It's her job. But for now, I want to keep what I know close. I'm not sure why. Instinct, I guess.

"My officer found a sleigh bell next to the body," she continues.

"I noticed."

"A bell from the bar. Did you drop it?"

"No."

"Did the owner of the bar drop it?"

I was afraid she'd ask that. "Anybody could have dropped it last night, or two days ago, or last week. The bell may mean nothing." Any competent defense attorney will surely make that point.

"Or the killer dropped it," she responds while I shrug.

"All right, Mr. O'Sullivan, I'm obviously not getting much out of you, but I may need to ask follow-up questions. Are you staying in town for the holidays?"

"Are you telling me not to leave town?"

"Calm down, Mr. O'Sullivan; I'm just wondering where I can reach you if I need to."

"I'll be here," I tell her as she hands me her card.

Dagnabit. I have to talk to Sammy. Now.

Chapter 5

After Scooby and I escape the cold embrace of the crime scene, I realize there's only one place to go—Dash's Diner. When I was a cop, it was a refuge of sorts where we could think through problems and hash out challenging cases with each other over a cup of coffee and a typical diner meal: eggs and bacon in the morning, meatloaf with mashed potatoes and Texas toast in the evening. We brainstormed, offered support, mulled over clues, and, in some cases, got a much-needed dose of cold reality.

I text Sammy and Jack.

Meet me at Dash's. ASAP. Urgent.

I prefer concise messages, a habit from years on the force where every word could be a clue, every pause a confession. I must admit, a benefit to these smartphones is the easy texting, allowing me to avoid the useless chatter of a phone call. *Hi, how are you? Good. How are you? I'm well. I think it's supposed to snow again this afternoon. Yeah, that's what the weatherman said on the news.* Phooey. My wife was so much better at handling those things. I like conversations quick and easy. Or not at all, if I'm being perfectly honest.

Within minutes, both Sammy and Jack respond with the same word.

Copy.

See? Quick and easy. It's like a spark of the old camaraderie, a reminder of days, when calls to action, were expected, and we always had each other's backs.

I slip the phone into my pocket, casting a final, lingering look over my shoulder at the community center, now swathed in yellow tape. The sleigh bell springs to mind again. Why does that keep popping into my head? Do I tell Sammy about it? And why does the thought of it make me uneasy? Anyone could have dropped that bell. There's no need to be uncomfortable about it. Yet Sammy's threat, *she'll regret this, and I'll make sure of it if it's the last thing I do*, haunts me. There's no way Sammy killed Ebenita, but I desperately wish he hadn't complained about her so loudly.

Dash's Diner is warm and cozy, a stark contrast to the biting cold outside. The bustling activity inside has steamed up the large front window, obscuring the slogan that reads *Where Most Get Their Toast*. I breathe deep, the scent of coffee and fried bacon surrounding me like a comforting blanket. From its classic checkerboard flooring to the gleaming chrome counter lined with red vinyl stools, I'd say this is my second favorite place next to the Veteran's Hearth Bar, of course. Scooby and I sit at our favorite table to wait for Jack and Sammy.

"Coffee?" a passing waitress asks.

"Yes, please." I nod as she pours me a cup and smiles at Scooby. I've never really asked if bringing my dog here is okay, but no one has thrown me out. Yet, anyway. Who will tell an old man that his dog isn't welcome? I know, 67 isn't that old, but I use it to my advantage when I can. Especially when it comes to Scooby.

Just as I finish my first cup of coffee, Sammy and Jack join us. They huddle together across from us, their somber expressions, and Sammy's startlingly unkempt appearance giving me pause. His usually neat, military-inspired grooming has given way to a wildly disheveled state. His hair, normally combed with precision, lies flat, while dark circles hang heavily under his bloodshot eyes, which are lacking their usual sharpness, dulled and clouded by the remnants of what? I don't know. I'm almost afraid to ask, but curiosity gets the better of me.

"Rough night?" I ask.

"You wouldn't believe it if I told you," he grumbles.

Jack shifts uncomfortably but remains silent.

"You've heard the news." I change the subject, looking back and forth between them.

Jack nods.

"It's all over the news," Sammy says, worry furrowed in his brow. "It's Ebenita, isn't it?"

"I'm afraid so."

"Let me guess, you saw the newscast and couldn't keep yourself away from the excitement," Jack suggests.

"Not exactly," I trail off.

"Uh oh. I don't like the sound of that," he responds.

"Oh, it gets better," I assure him.

They stare at me, awaiting my dramatic announcement.

"*I* found the body. Technically, Scooby found her."

Scooby barks to emphasize my point.

"How did you..." Jack looks like he's almost afraid to learn the truth.

"I didn't kill her!" I exclaim, inadvertently glancing at Sammy.

"Do the cops have any suspects?" Sammy asks, swallowing a large swig of the ice water in front of him. I notice his normally steady hand trembles slightly this morning.

"Not that I know of." I shake my head.

"What aren't you telling us?" Jack asks.

"Mind you, I don't think this means anything, but there was a bell from the bar beside Ebenita's hand."

"How do you know it was from the bar?" Sammy asks. "It's Christmas. The bell could have come from anywhere. A kid probably dropped it."

"It had the tag and the ribbon you put on the ones in the bar."

"Oh." He pauses, staring at me, steely-eyed. "Hold on a second. You're not saying you think it had something to do with me!"

"Of course not. You obviously didn't kill her. I'm just saying, don't be surprised if you catch some blowback for this."

"Who's working the case?" Sammy asks.

"Laura Rodriguez."

He nods thoughtfully. "She's a good detective."

"Ebenita, didn't just trip and fall and freeze to death?" Jack asks hopefully.

"I'm pretty sure she was strangled."

They cringe. We may be discussing a case. A case involving someone we didn't like. But no matter how mean Ebenita was, we knew her, and the thought of her being strangled and left in the snow is unnerving, to say the least.

"A lot of people made threats last night," Sammy points out hastily. "We all know that tons of people have threatened her over the years. Their suspect list must be lengthy."

Just as I start to respond, Jack interrupts. "Back up a second here. What were you doing at the community center this early in the morning?"

I was hoping they would overlook that. "I may have stopped at Ebenita's house to try to reason with her."

"Do the police know that?" Sammy asks.

"No, but it's only a matter of time."

"Why?"

"I left a note under her door asking her to reconsider."

"And you failed to mention that to the police?" Jack asks. "Did you lie to them?"

"I just left it out. They'll figure it out, eventually."

Sammy lets out a low whistle. "Not to be indelicate, but we can have the event now, right? Considering Ebenita's the one who got it canceled in the first place," he offers hopefully.

"It was the *City Council* that officially canceled our permit," I remind him, the bureaucracy of it all as bitter as the coffee we're sipping. "Remember, as someone pointed out last night - they're all on vacation until the first of January. No chance of overturning that decision now."

We pause as our waitress, a bright-eyed college student, serves our breakfast and refills our coffee cups. For several moments, the only sound at our table is the clinking of spoons against ceramic as we stir in cream and sugar and dig into our orders. Bacon, eggs, and pancakes for me. Huevos Rancheros for Sammy, and French Toast for Jack. Of course, I sneak a bite of bacon to Scooby when no one is looking. Okay, make it two. The diner continues to hum around us, the mundanity of others' breakfast routines providing an odd backdrop to our morbid conversation.

"Any other interesting tidbits you've neglected to mention?" Sammy asks.

"I took photos of the crime scene to study later. There were two sets of footprints. One was definitely Ebenita's boots; the other had a distinct shoe pattern, which I didn't recognize."

Jack leans back in his wheelchair, his gaze contemplative. "Maybe it's a sign, Howie. You should look into this. You've got the skills."

I shake my head vigorously. I knew this was coming. "I've hung up my hat, Jack. This is a job for the current badge holders. Detective Rodriguez is more than capable."

"But you're Howie!" he protests. "You've got a nose for sniffing out the truth. Or a dog who does." We all turn to look at Scooby, who waves his paw, asking for more bacon.

"Not this time," I insist.

"Then why go to her house to reason with her?" Sammy asks almost as if he's interrogating me.

"I didn't say it was a good idea," I respond. "This is Rodriguez case. I'm just..." I stop mid-sentence, unable to define what I am in this mess. Retired? Sure. But disinterested? Obviously not. Detached? I won't lie to myself. This mystery has its hooks in me, and I'm afraid, given our connection to the victim, it's only a matter of time before the other shoe drops.

Chapter 6

The diner door closes behind me with a soft thud, sealing in the patrons' murmurs and the toasty warm surroundings. As Scooby and I head for home, I shove my hands deep in my pockets, trudging on with thoughts of recent events, still weighing me down.

Last night, I was sure the worst thing that could happen was Ebenita's announcement that she finally got the children's Christmas event canceled. I was wrong. Her murder makes things far worse and the list of suspects is already as long as my arm including several of my friends.

Not that I believe any of *them* are capable of murder, but as a retired detective, I've seen more than my fair share of bizarre scenarios. There's accidental deaths where someone throws a punch or shoves a person who hits their head and dies. Sometimes, even a reasonable person snaps after years of torment. Then there's the deliberate planning and execution of a murder. But most are somewhere in between.

I doubt that Ebenita's death was premeditated, considering it wasn't even in her home. Now the question becomes, why were she and her killer at the community center? Was the meeting planned? My decades of experience tell me it wasn't a stranger. Did she fight back? Is there DNA? It was bitterly cold last night, so did the killer wear gloves? Given the condition of her body, I suspect it happened in the middle of the night. If only I could talk to the coroner like I did as an active detective.

The snow I failed to shovel earlier awaits us when we get home. Normally, that's something I do right away, but I was so distracted this morning that it slipped my attention. I put Scooby inside, where he happily waits, watching me from a fluffy blanket in the window seat.

Last night's snow only provided a light layer, making the shoveling easy. I keep mulling everything that's happened during the previous 24 hours. Less than 24 hours, actually. It would help so much if I knew what time Ebenita died. I still have friends in the coroner's office who I could contact on the sly. *But you're retired...* I remind myself.

Just as I finish shoveling, I'm surprised but delighted when my granddaughter Ellie pulls up to the house in her green Subaru, decorated with reindeer antlers and a red nose on the hood. I'm glad she isn't a curmudgeon like her Gramps. She's young, and it's Christmas. She *should* be cheerful. That idea dies, however, the second she sticks her head out of the car. "Gramps, I heard what happened. It's all over town," she scolds, her eyes wide with a mix of concern and natural curiosity. "Is it true? Ebenita Scroogina is dead?"

"Yes." I sigh in resignation. "It's true. And before you hear it from someone else, I found her body when I was out walking Scooby."

When her mouth hangs open in shock, I realize I've never seen her speechless.

"Let's go inside before Scooby loses his mind. I'll make cocoa and fill you in."

Having spotted Ellie through the window, Scooby barks wildly, whining to see her.

"I also heard they canceled the children's event. Why didn't you tell me?" she lectures.

"I promise I'll get to everything once we're settled," I insist while we stomp our snow-covered feet on the patio, scraping them on the rough welcome mat before going inside. In the entryway, I place our boots in the tray under the coat rack before hanging up our coats, hats, and scarves. I like everything to be orderly. It helps keep my mind settled.

"Scooby!" Ellie exclaims, her arms outstretched. Scooby races down the ramp we put by the window to protect his long back, nearly knocking it over in his excitement, before jumping into Ellie's arms, planting kisses all over her face.

I can't believe Ellie is in college now. Just last week, she was a toddler with pigtails wearing a mud-spattered pink dress (she was always playing outside and climbing trees), and now she's a young woman with a long, blonde ponytail and jeans with holes in them that she actually buys that way, which I'll never understand.

"How is his coat working out?" she smirks.

"You know very well it works great, and Scooby loves it. You're just rubbing it in."

"Yeah, I am."

"Put on an album while I make cocoa."

Ellie selects her favorite, Nat King Cole's *The Magic of Christmas*, which she has played so many times I'm surprised she hasn't worn it out. She carefully places it on my vintage turntable, patiently waiting for me to finish because she knows I can't talk and make cocoa at the same time. I make it the old-fashioned way, where I warm milk on the stove in a saucepan, add some cocoa powder and a generous helping of sugar, while finishing it with a dollop of whipped cream.

Ellie sits at the kitchen table worn from years of use; it bears the marks and scratches of countless family meals and conversations, each a silent witness to past laughter and discussions. My kitchen is a comforting mix of old and new. The cabinets, a faded shade of blue, hold an array of dishes and cooking utensils, some of which I fear are as old as Ellie. Framed family photos and Ellie's childhood drawings hang on the walls to tell the story of our history, a story deeply rooted in love and tradition.

After the cocoa heats to my satisfaction, I place a pair of mismatched mugs on the table and sit down. They're warm to the touch, a comforting contrast to the cold winter we left outside. Steam rises in gentle swirls, carrying with it the rich, sweet aroma of chocolate. With Christmas music playing softly in the background and Scooby sitting on Ellie's lap, for just a moment, I can almost forget everything that happened and just relish the experience.

We sip our cocoa while I fill her in on everything that has happened since Ebenita announced the cancellation of the Pedals of Promise event. Ellie asks many of the same questions that Jack and Sammy did, most of which I still can't answer yet.

"But you're investigating this, right?" she presses.

"Now you sound like Sammy and Jack. No. I'm not investigating. I'm retired, remember?"

"But you and Scooby found the body! How can you not investigate? I know you. I know you're already churning ideas around in your head."

"I may have taken a few pictures," I admit.

"Ah ha!"

"I only took pictures because I have that fancy phone you talked me into."

"Okay. Whatever you say."

"On to happier things. I'm considering a small Christmas tree. What do you think?"

Her face lights up, the shadow of the earlier conversation momentarily forgotten. "Really? That would be amazing! We could pick one out together! I bet Grandma's decorations are still in the attic. Unless you threw them out..." she hesitates.

"Of course, they're still there. But don't get all wacky on me. I'm not putting out a ton of decorations. Just a small, tasteful tree with a few lights."

As Ellie chatters on about her grandma's Christmas decorations, I smile. When she was little, the moment school let out for Christmas break, she'd demand her mother bring her right over so she and Grandma could add decorations to an already holiday-embellished house, bake cookies, and wrap presents.

"Sorry, Gramps, I gotta bounce," she announces suddenly, placing our empty mugs in the sink. "I have a shift at the bookstore this afternoon. I'm sure we'll be slammed with Christmas shoppers."

After she bundles herself up and says goodbye to Scooby, I promise we'll look for a tree in the next day or so. But just as I head back to the kitchen to put our mugs and the saucepan in the dishwasher, the doorbell rings. That kid. Always forgetting something.

"What did you forget this time?" I ask, throwing open the door with a flourish.

"I'm not sure?"

"Oh! I apologize, Detective Rodriguez; I thought you were my granddaughter. Come in. What can I do for you?"

"When did you plan to tell me about this?" she asks, brandishing an evidence bag with the note I left for Ebenita. "Or were you purposely hiding it from me?"

Chapter 7

"I didn't think it was significant," I claim. "It was merely a note to let her know I stopped by and wanted to talk to her about working on a solution for the Pedals of Promise event. Which you know already because you have it in your hand." I point to the evidence bag she holds at her side, hoping she isn't too angry with me for holding out on her.

She scowls. "You and I both know you purposely withheld that information."

"Would you believe me if I told you finding the body had me so rattled I forgot?" I fidget when Detective Rodriguez glares at me some more. She may be relatively short-statured and young, compared to me anyway, but she's intimidating. "I didn't think so," I mutter when she doesn't respond.

"We also have what I assume are *your* footprints leading away from Ms. Scroogina's home?"

"Those would be mine. Do you need to see my boots?"

She shakes her head, tucking a strand of hair behind her ear. "There was only one set of footprints this morning, so I'll take your word for it. For now, anyway," she adds. "Did you see any other footprints when *you* were at her house? Any signs of foul play?"

"No, but I wasn't looking either. If I'd realized I would find her body only a block away, I would have been more cautious. I didn't notice drag marks or signs of a struggle, although, again, I wasn't looking for them."

"Good to know," she says, scribbling notes in a small notebook.

"Do you have TOD?" I ask, not expecting her to share but hoping she might, anyway.

"Time of death was midnight."

Phew. Sammy was at the bar then. Not that I think he did it, but my gut tells me he'll need an alibi.

"I know Ms. Scroogina convinced the city council to cancel your charity event due to parking issues." Detective Rodriguez says.

"Yes."

"And she singled *you* out with the news at the Veteran's Hearth Bar."

"That she did."

"This is a big deal..."

"Yes, it is."

She sighs in frustration over my clipped answers. I can't help it. It's a habit.

"Do you know anyone who would want to harm Ms. Scroogina?" she asks.

"The entire town."

"How about narrowing that down a bit?" She rolls her eyes at me.

"Detective, as you're aware, Ebenita caused a lot of grief for many, many people in this town. For years! Do you know she once bragged to me about being a bully? She literally said, 'I'm a bully; that's how I get what I want.' Then she laughed. Who does that?"

Detective Rodriguez shoves her hands into her pockets. "Howie, I understand Ebenita was a troublemaker—big time. I assure you the department wasn't a fan. And that's putting it mildly. She'd show up at least once a week complaining about the tiniest infractions, insisting we arrest everyone from the neighbor who played his stereo too loud at a 4th of July barbecue to a six-year-old riding his bike past her house, ringing the bell on his handlebars. But that doesn't justify murder."

"I never said it did. I'm merely trying to emphasize that the list of suspects should be lengthy." I pause, wanting to ask her a thousand questions, but realize she's limited in what she can share about an ongoing investigation. But the worst she can say is no, right? "Did the coroner confirm she was strangled?" I blurt out.

She doesn't answer out loud, but the flash in her eyes tells me he did. "Do I have to warn you to stay out of the department's way and let us do our job?" she asks.

I raise my hands in surrender. "I'm retired. I don't need to butt in and cause trouble for you. I trust you, I respect you, and I have every confidence that you'll investigate this fully, ultimately bringing the killer to justice."

"I appreciate that," she says, her cheeks coloring slightly. Yes, even an old fogey like myself respects an accomplished detective - man or woman. "You'll let me know if you hear anything that could be relevant to this case?" she asks.

"Of course."

When she turns to leave, she pauses with her hand on the doorknob. "For what it's worth, I'm sorry she convinced the city council to revoke your event permit. I really don't know how or why she could do that, but I hope you figure out another way. It's a fantastic cause."

"Thanks, Laura, I appreciate it."

As the door closes behind her, I struggle to contain that familiar itch—the urge to solve the puzzle and to find the truth. It's an itch I was sure I'd learned to ignore. But as silence wraps around me, I consider how some parts of a detective never really retire—they simply wait for the right case to re-awaken them.

"C'mon, Scooby, let's go for another walk." We take the usual route where I often go when I need advice—Lisa's grave. I don't have flowers this time - they'd only wilt instantly in the cold, but I make a note to get a wreath for her headstone when we're tree shopping.

The snow crunches softly under our feet, a familiar Colorado sound, as we follow the winding path through the cemetery. A short distance away, the majestic Boulder Flatirons stand guard, their peaks dusted with snow, artfully contrasting against the blue sky.

Lisa's grave is in an especially peaceful corner of the cemetery, a spot that catches the afternoon sun just right. There's a bench nearby where I like to sit and think. The surrounding headstones are arranged in neat rows, with many decorated for the holidays—their thoughtful mementos adding a splash of color to the snow-covered landscape.

I like coming here. I hate the circumstances, but I like the place. I always experience a sense of calm, as if its natural beauty echoes Lisa's spirit.

I brush the snow off the top of her headstone when we arrive. "Hey, Lisa," I tell her. "You'll never believe this, but Ellie and I are getting a tree for me to decorate. Yes, me.

And Scooby says hi." Even Scooby seems to recognize the cemetery's significance when he spots a squirrel in a nearby tree but ignores it.

"I'll get right to the point," I start. I could never fool Lisa. It was useless to lie to her. Not that I ever needed to, though. "Ebenita Scroogina convinced the city council to revoke the permit for the Pedals of Promise event."

If Lisa were alive, she'd be livid. She would never have sat in stunned silence like I did when Ebenita handed me the letter. I dare say Ebenita would have ended up on the wrong end of that encounter. "But that's not the worst of it," I continue. "Ebenita was murdered last night. Someone strangled her. Scooby and I even found the body!"

For a second, I almost say that I'm surprised it took this long, but that would be inappropriate for a graveyard. No matter how mean Ebenita was. But, like everyone else in town, Lisa and Ebenita tangled several times. It's no surprise her death continues to cause problems. Perhaps even more than when she was alive.

"Here's the thing, and I haven't admitted this out loud to anyone else. I'm sure you remember how I always complain about Sammy's Christmas decorations, right? This year, he insisted on handing out these dopey sleigh bells to advertise the bar. They found one of the bells next to Ebenita's body. Not that I think Sammy did it or anything," I add quickly, "but it's not a good look at all. And when I met up with Sammy and Jack for breakfast this morning, Sammy looked like he went on a bender last night and slept on a park bench. But you know his history and that he rarely drinks anymore, so it can't be that.

"I hate that I'm having these thoughts," I tell her through clenched teeth. "I hate that this worries me. Now, everyone is nagging me to investigate. Well, everyone but Detective Rodriguez, of course. But I'm retired. I just can't put myself in the middle of this. Detective Rodriguez is the lead. She's a smart, talented young woman who's very good at her job, and I trust her to investigate this thoroughly. They don't need me. You'd like her, by the way. She transferred from Denver about a year ago. I hope the guys aren't giving her a hard time. I know how tough it can be for a woman on the force—especially a detective.

"But anyway..." I know I'm prattling on here, but it feels good to get my frustrations out, "she told me Ebenita was killed at midnight. As soon as she said that, I was relieved because that meant Sammy would have been at the bar working. But then I felt guilty for being relieved. On the one hand, I'm insisting no way Sammy did this, but on the other, I'm uneasy about how bad it looks."

"Besides, numerous people threatened Ebenita last night. They said harsh things about her after she left. Sammy was angrier than I've ever seen him. He even said he wouldn't be sad if she got run over by Santa's reindeer on her way home. I'm concerned that when Detective Rodriguez questions people who were in the bar, they'll recall the loud, obnoxious threats Sammy made.

"So, that's about it. Everything that's happened within the last couple of days. It's a lot, isn't it? Plus, I still have over two dozen bikes and families who I don't want to disappoint, but I haven't a clue how to fix it."

Suddenly, Scooby lets out a soft yip, drawing my attention. "What is it, boy?" I ask, following his gaze. He paws at something on the ground—a child's red mitten. "What have you got there?" I bend down beside him. "Good eye, Scoobs. I was so distracted I must have missed that earlier. Someone will be missing this."

I no sooner say that when a mother and her young son approach us, the boy's eyes light up as he points at us.

"There's my mitten!" he exclaims.

His mother smiles warmly. "Thank you for finding this. We've been looking everywhere!"

"Of course!" I tell her, handing it over. "Credit goes to Scooby here, though." I point at my dog who is now happily wiggling his tail as the little boy gently scratches his chin.

"Thank you, Scooby, you're a smart dog," Mom tells him.

I guess being that close to the ground has its advantages.

Scooby gives another quiet yip when my phone buzzes with a text. It's Ellie.

Are you at home? I'll pick you up so we can get a tree. Then you can buy me dinner.

I'm at your grandma's grave.

I'll be there in a jif!

Chapter 8

Ellie pulls up to the cemetery entrance, waving wildly, her cheeks flushed, her eyes sparkling with anticipation. She's more excited about this than I am. We buckle Scooby into the back seat in his special canine car seat, and off we go.

"Did you have a good talk with Grandma?" she asks.

"I did."

"Have you solved the murder yet?"

"I told you I'm not investigating this case."

"But you discussed it with her…"

She giggles when I refuse to respond. She knows me too well.

I assume Ellie isn't taking us to just any old tree lot. I shudder whenever I pass one of those unappealing lots on the street corner, the trees with brown needles and drooping branches. They look so sad and neglected. But the Evergreen Bliss Christmas Tree Farm, a family owned farm, on the west side of Boulder, isn't what I expected.

The festive sign at the entrance tells me they've been in business since 1954. During the holiday season, they offer sleigh rides, a hot cocoa stand, and handmade ornaments.

The moment we step out of the car, rows of festive evergreens highlighted with a dusting of snow greet us. It's a fragrant tapestry woven with the crisp, invigorating scent of pine, fir, and a hint of hot chocolate.

Ellie's laughter dances on the cold air as she practically skips from one tree to the next, her youthful exuberance a stark contrast to my more measured pace. I'm still unsure about this. Do I really need a tree? How much work will it be? Will I be sweeping up pine needles until February? What if it catches fire?

Just as I'm about to change my mind and tell Ellie this is a mistake, she shouts. "This one's perfect, Gramps!"

I follow her voice to find her jumping up and down, gesturing toward a robust Douglas fir whose branches stretch out in a welcoming embrace. I slide my hand over the soft needles, testing for freshness. "It's a bit tall, don't you think? I was picturing more like a tabletop tree."

"We'll make it fit. It has character, just like you," Ellie teases.

"How much is it?"

"You leave that to me," she says.

I'm pleasantly surprised as I listen to her negotiate with the farm owner; her bargaining skills a match for any seasoned investigator. It's in her DNA, after all. They finally settle on a price, and after I pay him, the clerk carefully cuts the tree, then hoists it onto the car roof before tying it down. Scooby circles us, barking and prancing with joy.

"He won't lift his leg on the tree, will he?" I ask.

"Gramps!" Ellie scolds.

"I'm the one who has to live with him."

"Scooby, you know the tree is for decorating and not for marking, don't you?" Ellie asks. Scooby agrees by bouncing up and down on his back legs.

After briefly returning to the cemetery to place the newly purchased fresh wreath on Lisa's headstone, I turn to Ellie. "Could we make another quick pit stop before dinner?"

"Sure, where?"

I hesitate before admitting this because I know how Ellie will react. "Starlight Community Center."

"I knew it!" she crows.

"You know nothing. I only want to stop there briefly. Indulge an old man's curiosity, would you?"

"Is there anything in particular we're looking for?" she asks as we cautiously make our way through the vicinity. The area surrounding the crime scene bears the chaotic stamp of multiple footprints crisscrossing in a haphazard pattern. The once pristine white canvas marred by evidence of the day's investigations - each step revealing a soundless story.

Long shadows stretch across the snow as the late afternoon sun dips toward the horizon, casting a somber mood. Fading light reflects off the compacted snow, the background eerily quiet while we circle the building, my practiced investigator's gaze sweeps the scene.

I'm sure the other investigators were thorough. But as I was reminded at the cemetery, things are often overlooked in the snow. I know that better than anybody. One of their newer investigators could have inadvertently stepped on something important, pressing it further into the snowpack.

"Gramps! Scooby found something!" Ellie calls out when Scooby barks out a signal.

Again? Please don't let it be another body. I find Ellie pointing at the ground in front of Scooby, a glint of metal shining near the snow-covered bush where we found Ebenita's body. Who knew my dog had a bit of bloodhound in him? Crouching down, I carefully brush aside a bit of snow, revealing a large brass key. I snap a picture before picking it up to get a better look. Custom-made I bet.

"Is it a clue?" Ellie asks.

"Hard to say," I murmur.

"Should we call the cops?"

"Not yet. Somebody could have dropped it here weeks ago," is my excuse for putting it in my pocket to study later. I'll turn it over to Detective Rodriguez without hesitation if I decide it's relevant. But I want to study it a little longer before turning it over. "I don't know about you, but I'm cold," I tell Ellie, hoping she won't notice the abrupt change in subject. "Are you ready for dinner?"

"Veteran's Hearth?" Ellie asks.

"Of course!"

"Howieeeee!" echoes the familiar refrain. Followed by "Scooby!" and a bark and then "Ellieeeeee!"

I feel better already, embraced by the familiar warmth of the bar and the enticing scent of a home-cooked meal. Okay, maybe not exactly home-cooked, considering we're in a bar, but Joe the chef is world-class, especially for an aging bar where a bunch of veterans hang out.

We settle at the usual table, where Jack is already waiting for us. Ellie chatters on to him about her final exams while I listen, or rather, I try to listen, but my mind is half on her and half on the key in my pocket. I'll have to turn it over to Detective Rodriguez eventually—just not this second. Besides, it may mean nothing, I reason with myself.

"What can I get for you folks? Nice to see you, Ellie," Bonnie greets us.

"I'll have the meatloaf and mashed potatoes…" I start before catching Ellie's eye. "And a side salad."

"A side salad? You feeling okay?" Jack asks.

"Ha ha. Very funny. I always have a side salad."

Ellie rolls her eyes when she sees Jack's shocked face. Like her grandmother, there's no fooling her.

"I'll have a grilled cheese sandwich and tomato soup, please," she tells Bonnie.

"Joe wants to know what the deal is with the side salad," Bonnie snorts when she returns with our orders. I thought these people had my back. Why must they rat me out like this?

Sighing with satisfaction, I dig into my mashed potatoes. Creamy and smooth, bathed in a rich, savory gravy, they're the perfect blend of comfort and buttery softness, melting delightfully on my tongue. When I catch Ellie staring at me, however, I spear a bright red cherry tomato from the top of my salad before popping it into my mouth. "Mmmm, good." I nod at her.

I appreciate feeling so comfortable, yet I can't help but recall a similar sensation last night, right before Ebenita burst through the door with her bad news. One moment, the children's event was on track, and everything was in order; the next, it was belly up.

Tonight, the children's event is still canceled. Ebenita is dead. And I worry for those of us who were Ebenita's loudest critics. Still, I enjoyed Christmas tree shopping with Ellie, and dinner is delicious, as always. Perhaps she'll agree to share some kind of dessert.

Then we can go home to put up the tree. I don't know what we'll do for Christmas this year. We'd planned to spend the day at the event, of course. Ellie's parents are in Barbados for the holiday, so it will just be us. I guess we'll spend it at home. Maybe Sammy and Jack would like to join us.

I'm convinced, however, that I cursed us all with my doubts when the door opens, and in walks Detective Rodriguez, flanked by uniformed officers. This is so not good. The bar falls silent, all eyes turning toward the officers as they make a beeline for Sammy.

"Samuel Thompson, you are under arrest for the murder of Ebenita Scroogina," Detective Rodriguez announces, the formal words jarring in the homely setting.

Some patrons gasp, some murmur swear words, while others don't bother murmuring; they just curse. Loudly. Me? I'm too stunned to say anything out loud. How could this possibly happen two nights in a row?

Sammy's face is a mask of shock and confusion. "This is a mistake," he stammers. "You've got the wrong person. I swear."

My heart sinks as I watch the officer read my old friend his rights. "Detective Rodriguez, what is going on here?" I ask, approaching the officers.

She turns to me, her expression grim. "I'm sorry, Mr. O'Sullivan. We have witnesses who place him at the victim's house shortly before the murder. He was pounding on the front door, shouting that she'd pay for what she'd done."

Chapter 9

"Jack, do something. You're a lawyer," I howl in protest.

"I'm an Intellectual Property lawyer," he reminds me. "He needs a criminal defense attorney, but I can fill in for now," he explains, rapidly wheeling his way over to the police and Sammy.

He better be telling him to keep quiet. As a cop, I always wanted them to sing like a bird. As a friend, I want him to keep his trap shut. No fruitless attempts at explaining whatever he thinks is a good excuse. Suspects often give long-winded stories because they're convinced the cops will suddenly throw up their hands and declare *if only we'd known; sorry to have wasted your time*!

Detective Rodriguez wouldn't arrest him without a good reason, which scares the daylights out of me. It's circumstantial evidence, no doubt, but knowing her, she's sure she has the right guy. Even though *I* know she doesn't.

The sleigh bell is undoubtedly part of it, but a good defense attorney will explain how anyone could have left it there. Unfortunately, Sammy's fingerprints will be all over it. See, I knew he shouldn't have handed out those dumb things.

Then I remember the key in my pocket and realize I need to say something. "Excuse me, Detective Rodriguez, I have—"

"You can see your friend at the courthouse after he's been processed," she cuts me off, right before whisking him out the door.

I could press the matter, but I don't. I want to study this key some more.

"Did you tell them he has an alibi?" I ask Jack as we return to our table. "Detective Rodriguez told me Ebenita was killed at midnight. Sammy was at work then. There will be witnesses from the bar! What is it?" I demand when Jack flinches.

"He closed the bar early last night."

"Early? How early?"

"Around 10 p.m."

"Why?" I'm so upset I'm almost shrieking my questions.

"Business was painfully slow. After the drama with Ebenita, the lousy weather, and the typical holiday slowdown, he decided it wasn't worth it and closed for the night."

"That's why Detective Rodriguez said neighbors saw him at Ebenita's house," I moan, dropping my head in my hands.

"I would assume so."

"You told him not to say a word?"

"I did. I also called a partner at my firm, and he'll meet them at lockup. He's the best criminal defense lawyer in Boulder."

"Someone needs to close the bar for him," I point out.

"I can do it," Bonnie says.

Jack plants his hand on my shoulder. "This is why you need to be involved. You know Sammy, the bar, the regulars, you know who tangled with Ebenita and when. I trust you to sort this out."

I sigh deeply. The weight of the world even heavier than before. "I know."

"Let's get you and Scooby home, Gramps," Ellie says softly. She and Jack don't even point out they knew all along I'd have to investigate.

A heavy silence hangs in the car for the short drive home, broken only by the soft hum of the engine and the intermittent swish of the windshield wipers against the softly falling snow. I sit slumped in my seat, my eyes staring blankly out the window. A turmoil of emotions, from confusion to sadness, churns inside me. Ellie grips the steering wheel, her knuckles whitening, a deep furrow of concern etching her brow. Occasionally, I glance at her, wanting to offer reassurance, but words fail me.

Once we're home, we carry the tree inside, with only a small trail of pine needles leading to the living room, so I take that as a good sign I won't have a big mess to worry about later. As if that's even a problem I should be concerned about right now. Together, we heave the tree into a stand I found in the attic this afternoon, adjusting the bolts at the bottom until it stands straight and proud.

"We'll decorate it later," I tell Ellie, brushing my hands together as if clearing them of more than just physical debris. "Right now, we need some sleep." Even though I know I won't sleep tonight. But I don't feel like decorating a tree while my best friend is being booked for murder at the county jail. "I've got a long day ahead of me tomorrow."

Ellie eyes me carefully, reflecting the gravity of the challenge before us. "*We've* got a long day. You have a lot of friends, and you have me. You won't have to do this on your own. And you'll clear Sammy's name, Gramps. I know it as sure as I'm standing here."

I promised Ellie I'd *try* to sleep, and I did. For all of three minutes. Instead, I spend most of the night pacing in the dark like I used to when working on a tough case, the day's events replaying in my mind on a loop. The key, the sleigh bell, the bar, and the supposed neighbors' claims roll around in my head like numbered bingo balls in a tumbler as I try to make sense of it all. Only no one is picking them out, one by one, to put them in order.

I'm not as worried about the sleigh bell or the key as I am about the witnesses. Are they sure it was him, and how? Is it him, or just someone who looks like him?

And what about that darn key? They could charge me with evidence tampering if it's part of the crime scene. If it isn't, and some passerby happened to drop it weeks ago, then I could look like I'm trying to hide evidence because I secretly think my friend is guilty. What if the key exonerates him? How I hate this! Didn't I tell them I'm retired?

Eventually, morning light creeps through the curtains, casting a soft glow on the untrimmed tree. My priorities are apparent: clear a good man's name, catch a killer, and create a Christmas miracle for needy kids and their families. No problem.

Chapter 10

This morning is like all mornings. Scooby runs outside to do his business while I make coffee. Only this morning, I have to solve the mystery of who killed Ebenita Scroogina and get my best friend out of jail. And I still don't know what to do for the Pedals of Promise kids and their families.

But first, we get Sammy released on bail. Of all the weeks to get arrested for something he didn't do, days before Christmas is the worst because most people at the courthouse are gone for the holiday, so the process will move even slower than usual.

I texted Jack in the middle of the night, inviting him and his law firm partner to my house bright and early to discuss Sammy's case. I'm pleased, yet not surprised when the doorbell rings precisely on time. Jack is a stickler for punctuality.

"Gentlemen, come in. Would you like some coffee and rum cake? I just put on a fresh pot."

"Rum cake? You made rum cake?" Jack asks skeptically.

"Ellie made it if you must know," I admit. "Greg." I nod at the criminal defense lawyer. Gregory Kaplan and I were often on opposite sides of the law and butted heads in court regularly when I was a detective. But if anyone is representing Sammy, I'm glad it's him. He's very good. Too good, I've often thought.

Scooby, convinced they're here to see him, dances at their feet, barking his greeting until they each pause to say hello, rewarding him with head scritches.

"The other day, my wife came back from the grocery store and tells me she saw a fella with a sausage dog wearing a red coat in the produce section. I assume that was you?" Greg laughs. His soft southern accent adding to the humor.

"Undoubtedly." I nod. "My granddaughter's idea. So, tell me. How bad is it?" I ask, placing steaming coffee mugs and cake in front of them on the kitchen table.

Greg grimaces. "I'm making every effort to get him out as soon as possible, but as you're well aware, this isn't the ideal time to get arrested. This time of year the courts are about as useful as a screen door in a submarine."

"*Is* there an ideal time to get arrested?" Jack asks, looking perplexed.

"Not Christmas!" Greg and I exclaim in stereo.

"Judge Benson is working with a skeleton staff until after New Year's Day," Greg points out. "They're processing the cases as expeditiously as possible, but it's still slow. The City Attorney owes me a favor, so I hope to call that in to get Sammy released. Given that Sammy's a veteran, a small business owner, and an upstanding community member, I have every reason to believe they'll release him on his own recognizance."

"What does the case look like?" I ask. Once I know what we're facing, I can build a case around how Sammy *couldn't* have done this. *I* know he couldn't have, but now I need to prove it.

"You already know about the sleigh bell, which, of course, has his fingerprints on it."

"Anyone could have dropped that," I point out.

"Which is what we'll argue. Fortunately, it wasn't on her body or in her hand. It was simply near her, so that should help with a jury - if it gets that far. There's also the unfortunate fact that numerous witnesses at the bar overheard Sammy say he would love to see her run over by a reindeer on her way home. And that was one of the milder things," Greg reminds us, shoveling another bite of cake into his mouth.

"A lot of us said disparaging things about Ebenita. Me included," I confess.

"Me too." Jack raises his hand.

"Right. And I plan to use that to our advantage."

"Is it true, though? Sammy closed the bar early? He never does that," I ask, hoping I got that part wrong.

"Yes sir, it's true," Greg says, while Jack nods sorrowfully.

"And there's neighbors who saw him at Ebenita's?" I press, clinging to the irrational hope that if I ask enough times, the answer will change somehow.

"Yes. And I'm aware the police have questioned you already, about your visit to Ebenita's house, Howie," Greg says, "but did you see anything out of the ordinary? Something you only recently remembered."

Like the telltale heart, the key in my pocket reminds me of its presence. Thump. Thump. Thump. The longer I wait to say anything, the worse it will look, but I still can't say it out loud. I only need a little more time to study it. I shake my head adamantly. "I saw no evidence of foul play at her house. It appeared to be locked tight, no jimmied door jamb or broken windows."

"Footprints?" he presses.

I sip my coffee before answering. "The only new footprints there were mine. Given the evidence we know of so far, experience tells me she was killed at the community center and not at her house. Did they find DNA on her?"

"I don't have all the discovery yet. They're supposed to deliver more to my office this afternoon, but my sources tell me there's no DNA under her fingernails and no scratch marks or bruising anywhere on Sammy."

"So there's that, at least." I breathe a sigh of relief. "But back to the neighbors."

"Yes sir," Greg leans forward. I've obviously hit on something unusual. "Here's where it gets interesting. One neighbor insists she saw him at 11:00—"

"Before Ebenita was killed." I interrupt.

"Yes, but another neighbor swears it was 1:00 a.m.," Greg adds.

"So, he was there twice?" Jack asks, confusion etched across his face.

"Or one of the witnesses has the time wrong," I point out. Witnesses often tell different stories—even witnesses who were standing next to each other.

"Exactly," Greg says.

"Exactly to which scenario?" Jack asks.

"Both!" Greg and I exclaim in unison. This is becoming a habit.

"Where did Sammy say he was?" I ask.

Greg and Jack shoot each other a look that immediately arouses my suspicions. "What?"

Jack fidgets in his seat. "After you left, Sammy started drinking."

"Oh boy." I shake my head. After Sammy retired from the Army, he drank. A lot. He also got into trouble. Nothing too serious, but one night in the bar, a drunk patron was making unwanted passes at some women. Sammy, who also had too much to drink, scuffled with the guy. Chairs were broken, and the cops were called. Other than a few bumps and bruises, no one got hurt, but it was a wake-up call for Sammy, who realized how quickly things could get out of control in a bad way. After that, he cut way back. I can't remember the last time I saw him drink to excess. I rarely see him drink at all.

"It's my fault," Jack laments.

"How is it your fault?" I ask.

"When I realized he was drunk, I insisted he give me his car keys. He promised me he'd sleep it off on the pull-out couch in the back room. I should have insisted he come home with me. Then he would have had a foolproof alibi."

"He confirmed he slept it off in the bar?"

"Not exactly." Greg's lengthy pause makes me nervous. "He says he doesn't remember what happened."

"Not much of an alibi, then." After scribbling some notes in my notepad. I groan. "I'm acting like I'm still a detective here."

"You'll always be a detective, won't you?" Jack smiles.

"But I won't have the access to witnesses and records that I once did. And Detective Rodriguez has already warned me not to interfere. I've given that speech myself more than once to wanna-be true crime fans who were so sure they knew how to conduct a proper investigation."

It annoys me when Greg and Jack give each other yet another conspiratorial look. "What is this?" I wave my hand between them. "I feel like you were plotting before you ever got here."

"I want to hire you," Greg says.

"Hire me? I'm not a lawyer."

"Not as a lawyer. As an official investigator for the firm. It will give you some leeway. Make you a little more official."

"What part about retired didn't you get? I'm far too old to be starting a new career."

Greg raises his hand. "Don't get your feathers ruffled. We often hire retired cops. They're a perfect fit for the job. Besides, it's temporary. Just for this case, I swear."

"Do it for Sammy," Jack urges.

"All right. But only for this case."

"Fair enough," Greg says.

"All right!" Jack shouts, prompting Scooby to run in circles and bark.

Why do I feel ganged up on here?

Chapter 11

It would be easier if I had the witness list in my hands, but I refuse to wait, even if Greg expects it this afternoon. I have to move quickly to clear Sammy's name, so waiting on a courier who, for all we know, is drinking cocktails at the office Christmas party doesn't work for me.

Besides, after 25 years on the force, I can pretty much guess which neighbors talked to the police. It's the same on every block. Certain neighbors refuse to speak with the authorities because they're convinced *someone will come after them*. (Although they're never clear on who this someone is.)

Then there's the neighbors who are always vigilant, keenly aware of who's coming and going on their block, eager to provide detailed accounts of local activity. And with the rising popularity of inexpensive home security cameras, many have access to valuable footage, capturing critical moments and evidence—all in the palm of their hands!

Scooby and I assume we'll attract attention if we hang out near Ebenita's house long enough. I don't want to look like I'm casing the block, but Scooby should ease those fears. We select a house next door to Ebenita's first because she has a neighborhood watch sign in her yard among the Christmas decorations. I try to look lost, yet not too creepy. Sure enough, after a moment, there's a pleasantly round, gray-haired lady peeking at us through the front window. I wave, but she disappears. Then reappears several seconds later, so I wave again.

"Can I help you with something?" she asks, opening her front door.

"Hi there," I exclaim, slowly approaching the patio. "I'm retired Detective Howie O'Sullivan, and I just have a few questions about your neighbor, Ebenita Scroogina."

"Hello there. I'm Irene Jensen, do come in. My stars, your little dog is adorable."

"Can he come in with me?" If she says no, we'll have to talk outside. I won't leave Scooby alone in the cold.

"Of course! I love his jacket."

Mrs. Jensen is a sprightly woman. Eighty-something, I'll guess. One step into her home, and the scent of gingerbread and cinnamon transports me to a simpler time, surprising me with a pang of nostalgia. A time when my wife was alive and Ellie's mom was little. What is happening to me? First, a Christmas tree, and now I'm a little more choked up than I'd like to admit over the smell of baked goods. Am I getting soft in my old age?

"I understand you saw someone at Ebenita's house the night she was murdered?" I ask, taking a chance it was her.

"Oh my, yes," Mrs. Jensen says, placing a hand against her chest. "I heard an awful ruckus over there. When I looked out the window, I saw a man wearing a heavy leather jacket and a gold hat pounding on Ebenita's door at 11:00," she recounts, adjusting her glasses. "He was furious, and I could tell he was drunk. He kept shouting something about needy children, I think? He told Ebenita she had to come out and face the music because he was tired of her terrorizing the town."

"And you're sure about the time?" I confirm.

"Absolutely, Mr. O'Sullivan," she nods enthusiastically. "I remember looking at my bedside clock, and it said 11:00. I said, 'Lester, what is that fool doing out at 11:00 on a night like this?'"

"Lester? Is that your husband?"

"Yes. Sixty-three years next May," she says proudly.

I scribble notes, nodding. "Did you notice when the man left?"

"No," she admits. "But he wasn't here long. I made a quick trip to the bathroom. That's how it is when you get to be my age. When someone wakes you up in the middle of the night, you might as well go to the bathroom. When I returned, I was going to call the police, but I looked out the window, and he was gone. What is this world coming to these days? I swear it gets crazier and crazier. You know, just the other day..."

While she chatters on, a large orange tabby cat wanders around the corner, freezing when he sees Scooby. Scooby is about the size of a small cat, give or take, but this cat is one hefty feline. Bigger than Scooby by several pounds. His eyes narrow as he stares down this unexpected dog in his living room.

Scooby, who's never met a cat, is unsure how to react. At first, he wags his tail nervously, but not the way he does when he sees someone he knows, and the tail wags him. This is short and close to his body. When the cat marches over to us, Scooby tries to hide behind me while Mrs. Jensen continues waxing poetic about world affairs.

Meanwhile, I'm worried this cat is about to eat my dog for lunch. He sniffs Scooby up one side and down the other, no doubt wondering why a coat-wearing dog has dared to come into his house. Before I can react, he smacks Scooby on top of the head, who barks while scratching frantically at me to be picked up. I reach down and grab Scooby before we have a brawl on our hands.

"Mr. Pickles!" Mrs. Jensen scolds. "Is that how we treat a guest?"

I'm sure if Mr. Pickles could talk, he would tell her that's exactly how one treats a canine guest. He throws Scooby one more disgusted look before stalking away, his tail straight in the air.

"I understand that another neighbor saw Sammy as well?" I ask, cradling a shivering Scooby, grateful for the excuse to get back to the investigation.

"Yes, that would be Mr. Kowalski, the retired mailman across the street."

"I really appreciate your time, but we should go," I apologize before Mrs. Jensen can launch into another speech about current events.

"What did you say your name was again young man?" she asks.

"Howie. Howie O'Sullivan. I'm a retired detective but temporarily working as an investigator for Baxter, Sterling & Dunn."

"You can't leave empty-handed. Let me send you home with some gingerbread men. Is there a Mrs. O'Sullivan?" she calls out from the kitchen.

"There was. She passed away three years ago."

"I'm so sorry to hear that." She returns with a festively wrapped package of cookies. "You come back any time, you hear? I hope your little dog is okay."

"I'm sure he'll be fine," I tell her while Scooby sniffs the cookies, the incident now mostly forgotten with the possibility of scoring a tasty treat.

"Oh, look, Mr. Kowalski is shoveling his walk." She points out while opening the door for us. "You can ask him now."

Scooby nervously looks over his shoulder at Mr. Pickles, who is now perched on the back of the couch, grooming himself while looking quite satisfied.

I place Scooby back on the ground now that he's safely away from Mr. Pickles, and we cross the street toward the snow-shoveling neighbor; the rhythmic scrape of metal on concrete cutting through the quiet neighborhood.

Mr. Kowalski appears to be in his late 70s, a sturdy man with a head of thick silver hair combed to the side and a deeply lined face, no doubt from his years spent working outdoors in the sun. He's wearing an old postal service coat, a thick scarf, and heavy gloves.

"Hi, Mr. Kowalski?"

"Yes."

"My name is Howie O'Sullivan, and I'm investigating your neighbor's death."

"Oh. Yeah. You a cop?"

"I'm retired. But I'm working for Baxter, Sterling & Dunn temporarily. Mrs. Jensen," I turn to point at her house where she's still watching us and waving, "said you may have seen something the night Mrs. Scroogina was killed."

"Yep. I saw a man. Heard him, too. Made quite a racket. Hard to miss, even with my hearing."

"Can you describe him?"

"Older dude. Army. Wearing a leather bomber jacket and a gold Army veteran ball cap."

Unfortunately, they've both accurately described Sammy. "What time did you see him?"

"1:00 a.m."

Greg was right. Two different times. "Are you sure about the time?" I ask.

"As sure as the snow is cold," he grumbles. "Why? Someone else say different?"

I respond only with a grunt, my mind racing. Two neighbors, two sightings of Sammy, each adamant about the time, yet two hours apart. Was Sammy really here twice? Once before and once after Ebenita was killed? What if the prosecution argues that Sammy showed up at 11:00, killed Ebenita at midnight, then came back a second time at 1:00 to make it look like he hadn't killed her earlier?

"May I ask how you're certain it was 1:00 a.m.?"

"I was waiting for Neptune to set."

He pauses as if I'll know precisely what he means by that. "Neptune?" I finally ask.

"Yes. I have a telescope. Neptune sets just after 1:00 a.m."

"I see. What was the man saying?"

"He was drunk as a skunk and angry. Kept shouting how Ebenita was going to pay for what she'd done. You know, if you're investigating her murder, you should talk to Larry Bennett on the other side," he insists, pointing to the house on the south side of Ebenita's. "He and Ebenita had some vicious fights about one of his trees hanging over her property. She insisted the roots were causing damage to her sewer line and her driveway. She repeatedly threatened to sue him."

"Did she ever follow through on it?"

"Beats me." He shrugs.

An ongoing and expensive lawsuit could be a motive for murder. This sounds promising. "Thanks. I appreciate your help," I tell him.

"Anytime," he says, giving me a curt nod before returning to his shoveling.

"Looks like we're visiting with one more neighbor, Scoobs."

After I ring the doorbell, a large man with a thick beard and stern face answers, eyeing me warily. I can't help but think how easily he could strangle someone.

"Mr. Bennett?" I clear my throat. "My name is Howie O'Sullivan, and this is Scooby," I nod at Scooby as if it wouldn't be clear who I'm talking about. Scooby responds with a firm bark. He's undoubtedly hoping there are no large, mean cats lurking around the corner at this house. "I'm investigating what happened to your neighbor, Ebenita. Do you mind if I ask a few questions?"

Bennett sighs. "I heard about Ebenita. Terrible business, that. What do you want to know?"

"How well did you know her?"

"Well enough to dislike her," he replies with gruff honesty. "She was a nightmare. Always complaining about my trees. She even threatened to cut them down herself. Tried to sue me too."

"And where were you last night, Mr. Bennett?"

Bennett's face flushes. "I was at work. Patty's Pot Emporium I work the night shift."

"What time did you get home?"

"12:30."

"Did you see or hear anything unusual that night? After you got home from work, I mean?"

"Nope." He shakes his head.

"Okay, thank you for your time."

"No problem," he grumbles before shutting the door abruptly.

That makes two neighbors who swear they saw Sammy at different times and one neighbor, who I consider a suspect, who saw and heard nothing, even though he arrived home shortly before Mr. Kowalski claims *he* saw Sammy. At least one of them is mistaken or lying. My money's on lying.

Chapter 12

Scooby and I pause on the sidewalk to scribble additional notes in my notepad, but just as we're about to move on, the familiar purr of a well-maintained police cruiser rolls up. Hell's bells. Busted already.

Detective Rodriguez steps out of the cruiser, her posture still exuding the authority that has men twice her size straightening their backs and mumbling 'ma'am.' What is it about this petite woman that always makes me nervous? I fear it's real—I *am* getting soft in my old age. She fixes me with a stern look as she approaches.

I stuff my notebook into my pocket and face her, mustering my best apologetic smile. "Greetings, Detective."

"Why am I not surprised to find you here?" she asks. "Don't tell me you're interfering in an active investigation."

"I'm acting as an investigator for Baxter, Sterling & Dunn. I'm not breaking the law by talking to people, after all. Can't a man socialize?"

Detective Rodriguez folds her arms, unamused. "Socializing is one thing. Interfering with a police investigation is another. The entire department is on edge, and I don't need civilians muddying the waters. Anything you find, you're expected to share. Immediately."

I nod, understanding firsthand the position she's in. "I've found nothing worth mentioning," I lie, the words tasting like ash in my mouth. It's not a colossal lie. She already knew about the neighbors, and the key I found may have nothing to do with this case. *Then why don't you just show her*, the little voice in my head chastises me. *Because it **could** have something to do with this case*, I bite back at myself.

"Mrs. Jensen and Mr. Kowalski told me the same thing they told you. They saw a man fitting Sammy's description at Ebenita's house at 11:00 and 1:00."

"What do you make of that?" she asks.

"Isn't it your job to figure it out?" I ask a little more abruptly than I should.

When she pinches her lips in frustration, I realize that sounded mean spirited.

"I apologize. I'm concerned for my friend, who I *know* didn't kill Ebenita, and being on the civilian side of an investigation is new to me. But you and I both know witnesses often give conflicting accounts."

"I do." She nods. "But a two-hour difference is a lot."

"I agree. I also talked to Mr. Bennett, the neighbor on the other side," I swivel to point in that direction, "but he was at work until 12:30, and saw nothing unusual after arriving home."

At this, her gaze softens slightly, and she sighs, the sound lost in the winter air. "I know you mean well, Howie. But this is my case. My responsibility. If you get in the way, it's not just *your* hide on the line—it's mine too." The worry lines etched into her brow are a subtle sign of a sleepless night, just like mine. I know that look all too well; the look of a case that gets under your skin and won't let go.

"I understand," I assure her.

She holds her gaze a moment longer as if she's searching my face for the earnestness of my promise. "We know this isn't a game. It's an active investigation; if you cross too many lines, you risk compromising the entire case."

I feel a twinge of guilt for refusing to tell her about the key, knowing full well the potential significance it could hold. I have to tread carefully here, aware that my unofficial inquiries might ruffle feathers—or worse. When the time is right, I'll turn over everything to the authorities. After all, the best way to keep from stepping on toes is to ensure I'm always one step ahead.

"I'm after the truth," I assure her. "You know as well as I do that sometimes it takes a bit more than just following protocol."

She sighs, pinching the bridge of her nose. "And you also know that 'a bit more' can lead to tainted evidence, which could, in the end, hurt your friend more than it helps him. I can't have civilians, retired detective or not, complicating things. If you have information, Howie, bring it to me. Let me do my job."

When I nod, she gives me a final long and searing look. How many perps has she broken this way? Being on this side of the law is more uncomfortable than I would have predicted. With a bob of her head, she turns and walks back to her car, leaving Scooby and me standing on the sidewalk, my mind a whirlwind of jumbled thoughts.

"Okay, Scooby. It's on to the locksmith," I tell him while we watch Detective Rodriguez drive away. I desperately hope I'm doing the right thing here. Scooby's loud bark tells me he thinks I am. At least, that's how I interpret it.

The bell above the door jangles when I step into the musty

interior of Jasper's Lock & Key, a small shop on a street that has seen better days, tucked between a bakery and a laundromat. The shop is a throwback to a different time, its walls lined with keys of all shapes and sizes, padlocks, and thick, leather-bound dusty books on locksmithing.

A man, who I assume is Jasper, stands behind a cluttered counter wearing a magnifying headpiece, peering over an intricate lock mechanism. He looks up as I approach—his magnified eyes comically large before he flips the headpiece up with a practiced motion.

"Retired cop?" he asks.

"That obvious?" I respond.

"Only to someone like me." He laughs. "It's my job to notice tiny details."

"I found this key, and I'm curious about it." I'm embarrassed that my hand is almost, but not quite, trembling when I hand it over. I'm not used to being so personally involved in a case.

"Let's see what you've got here," he murmurs, examining it under a bright lamp. His eyes light up as he runs his fingers over it, the tactile memory of a thousand keys aiding his inspection.

"It's an old one," he insists, "handcrafted, not one of those mass-produced pieces you normally see. These cuts are precise and intentional. It's meant for a custom lock—likely a cabinet or a chest. Something special, something worth securing."

"Any idea who could make this? Are they nearby?" I ask.

He nods, his gaze distant as he dredges up the information from the recesses of his memory. "There's an artisan steelworker who goes by the name of Alastair McClellan. Bit of a hermit, but he's the kind who'd craft this and the lock. His work is almost like a signature—unique, unmatched." He continues to speak in a staccato tone.

"Where can I find him?"

"Last I heard, he still has a workshop in Gunbarrel," Jasper replies, handing back the key. "Follow the old forest road until it's no longer paved. There's a wooden sculpture of a bear out front with several No Trespassing signs."

"That's perfect. Thank you." I smile, gratefully.

Jasper leans in closer, his voice dropping to a coarse whisper that prickles the back of my neck. "Be careful, mister. Alastair's a reclusive man, wary of strangers. And there are rumors. Strange ones about his work."

I tighten my grip on the key, its cold metal feeling heavier by the moment. My mind churns with possibilities while the warning about Alastair McClellan echoes ominously. "I appreciate the tip," I tell him. "One more thing..." I start, unsure if I should even say it out loud.

"I get it. We never talked," he grunts.

"Thanks, man." I dip my head in appreciation before returning outside to the cold Colorado day.

Chapter 13

Before I can decide my next move, my phone buzzes with a text message from Greg,

The judge denied bail for Sammy.

How is that possible? Can he have visitors?

Yes. Visiting hours start in 20 minutes.

The judge denied bail? I don't understand it. How could he deny bail for someone like Sammy? This snag makes it more critical than ever that I solve this case quickly.

I also know the one place that will refuse to overlook Scooby's presence is the county jail. Besides, he doesn't want to visit the jailhouse anyway. Thankfully, Ellie loves spending time with him and assures me they'll use the time to start decorating. I remind her to keep it simple, but I suspect she'll ignore my request.

The heavy, overcast sky looms over the county jail, providing an appropriate backdrop for the depressing setting. County lockup is a patchwork of utilitarian concrete blocks and narrow windows secured by robust bars. Inside is a labyrinth of sterile, echoing corridors, doors with peeling paint and rusting fixtures. The air is thick with a mix of disinfectant and stale confinement, resonating with the muffled echoes of inmates' and guards' voices.

Because of my longtime friendship with the guards, they let me visit Sammy in his holding cell instead of the noisy public visiting area. It's a small, bleak square with walls painted a color that might have once been white but are now dulled to a grimy gray. A cheap cot with a lumpy mattress and a scratchy blanket takes up much of the space. Beside it, a stainless-steel toilet and sink unit reflect the harsh fluorescent lights above.

After a restless night in lockup, Sammy is a shadow of his usual self. His customary, neatly combed hair is disheveled, with various strands falling haphazardly over his forehead. His unkempt beard adds to his weary expression. His usually vibrant eyes are dull, and the robust color that often marks his cheeks has drained away, leaving his skin sallow under the unforgiving lights. His posture slumps, the weight of his situation visible on his shoulders. The orange jail jumpsuit starkly contrasts his usual attire, making him seem even more out of place—an incongruous splash of color against the surrounding drabness.

A complex wave of emotions washes over me when I first observe my old friend in the grim confines of prison. First, it's a shock seeing someone I've known for so long and always associated with freedom and camaraderie caged within cold, unyielding walls. The shock quickly morphs into deep sadness at the harsh reality of his situation.

Then, there's a surge of helplessness and frustration. As a retired detective, I'm accustomed to being in control. I solve problems; I don't stand by them helplessly. Seeing my dear friend behind bars, unable to offer immediate help or solace, is heartbreaking.

Yet, there's a steadfast resolve underlying all of this, strengthening my determination to uncover the truth and do whatever I can to solve this mystery—a motivation fueled by loyalty, justice, and the enduring bond of our friendship. Despite the dismal setting and the grim circumstances, I'm more committed than ever to sort this out.

"I didn't do it!" are the first words from his mouth.

"I know you didn't," I assure him.

"So tell them that!" he gestures angrily at the world outside the prison.

"I have. And I'm working on proving it."

"How?" He dismisses me.

"Greg hired me to help his firm investigate."

Surprise flickers across his face, followed by profound relief. "What do you need from me?" he asks.

"I need to know everything. After Ebenita told us she convinced the city council to cancel the Pedals of Promise event, did you notice anyone at the bar who seemed particularly upset?"

"That was pretty much all of us," he reminds me.

"Yes, I get that. But is there anyone who stands out? Anyone who looked like they might do something regrettable? Someone who said something particularly outrageous?"

"You mean like me wishing I'd find her in the street after she was run over by Santa's reindeer?"

"To be frank, yes."

"Not one of my finer moments," Sammy laments.

"You were angry, I was angry, we were all angry. It's not an excuse, yet it's understandable, given the situation. We've all lived with Ebenita's abuse for years, and it felt like that was the last straw. It's one thing for her to argue with her neighbor over trees, but entirely another to cancel an event on purpose, causing children and their families heartache and grief. Do you recall anyone who showed an unnatural interest in the bells you were passing out?"

"Not that I noticed," he says, dragging his hands through his hair and shaking his head sorrowfully. "I'm so sorry I don't have more to tell you."

"That's okay. Keep going over that night in your mind; perhaps something will pop up later. They told me you closed the bar early."

Sammy nods. "After you left, the place thinned out. No one else came in, and Ebenita had already ruined the evening, so I shut it down. I was in a horrible mood, anyway."

"Jack said you were drinking."

"I don't know what got into me. You know I rarely drink these days. I'm so ashamed." Sammy hangs his head.

"I'm glad he took your car keys."

"Believe me, I'm extremely grateful he did. The outcome could have been far worse."

"Ebenita's neighbors can place you at her house that night."

He winces. "Yeah, Greg told me that."

"Why did you go to her house?"

"It's all very fuzzy. I only have a faint recollection of it."

"They say you were there twice."

"I swear I don't know how it happened. I vaguely remember pounding on her door and shouting at her to come out."

"Do you remember what time it was?"

"I really can't say for sure. I'm horrified I did it at all, but why would I go there twice?"

"Did you call a cab or a ride share? How did you get there?"

"This will sound weird, but I think I rode a bike."

"You rode a bike? In the snow? Do you even have a bike?"

"No."

"How did you ride a bike there?"

"I realize it sounds ridiculous. But a bike ride keeps popping into my head. Jack thought it sounded too bizarre, as well, so he's calling cab companies in the area to see if anyone has a record of picking me up. But I can't stop thinking about a bike ride."

"Let's just assume for a moment that you rode a bike to Ebenita's. Did you ride it back to your place? Did you wake up the next day to find a strange bike in your bar?"

"No. Not at all. There's no sign of a bicycle."

"I fear that the prosecution will claim you went to Ebenita's house, killed her, dragged her body to the community center, but went back to her house later to make certain you hadn't left any evidence behind. And that's why the neighbors saw you at two separate times. I need you to keep racking your brain over this. Even the smallest detail that jumps out at you could be important."

"Other than finding one of my bar decorations next to Ebenita's body and the neighbors who claim they saw me at her house, why does Detective Rodriguez think I killed her? It doesn't make sense."

The key weighs heavily in my pocket, and I consider asking Sammy about it, but that would mean admitting I could have crucial evidence on me.

"That's been bothering me too," I admit. "What motive does she think you have other than you and numerous others being angry? I'm certain something is missing here, so it's vital you remember. I need to determine what motive she thinks you had other than being upset about the children's event. Is there anything you aren't telling me? Something you'd know about Ebenita that I don't?"

"No. I swear you know everything I know. Or at least everything I can remember."

"Hey guys, sorry to interrupt, but visiting hours are over," a beefy-looking but polite guard tells us.

"Keep thinking, okay?" I tell Sammy, patting him on the shoulder reassuringly.

"We'll have you out of here in a jiffy." Now, if only I felt as confident as I'm trying to sound.

Chapter 14

My footsteps are unusually heavy when I leave the jail; the click of the door locking Sammy in still echoes in my ears. I've seen people behind bars before - plenty of times - but this is different. It's someone I know. Someone I believe to be innocent.

I fish my phone out of my pocket, typing a brief text to Ellie.

Heading home. Tree look good?

Her reply comes almost instantly, a stream of emojis that I assume means she's excited about Christmas, but it's hard to say. Still, it makes me smile. I'm always glad when Ellie is happy.

Scooby's more tinsel than dog. Pizza for dinner?

Sure. Nick-N-Willy's?

Yasss!

I call the pizza place, ordering our usual with an extra dash of red pepper flakes, just as Ellie likes. The irony isn't lost on me that if things had gone accordingly this week, I'd be at Veteran's Hearth reviewing our final plans for Pedals of Promise. Instead, the bar sits dark while Sammy is in jail for a murder he didn't commit. And I'm still burdened with not wanting to disappoint the children.

My next call is to Greg. I'm convinced that Sammy took a cab to Ebenita's. I can't imagine where he got the idea that somehow he found a bike in the snow and rode it. I don't care how drunk he was. The cab company would have the pickup time too, which could clear him immediately.

"Sorry, Howie," Greg sighs. "We've checked with every cab company in town, but only two had calls that night, and they weren't from Sammy and were nowhere near Ebenita's house. Sounds like everyone in town stayed home because of the weather."

I squeeze the phone in frustration. Another dead end. Another piece of the puzzle that doesn't quite fit. When I arrive home with the ready-to-bake pizza, pine smell and twinkling lights greet me. Lots of lights. And tinsel. And decorations covering every spare surface in the house.

Ellie has transformed the living room into a Christmas haven with Scooby, covered in silver tinsel, wagging his tail so hard it's almost wagging him. This isn't quite what I had planned... I just wanted a simple tree with a few lights... Oh well. Ellie and Scooby are happy, so that's what counts.

"Gramps is home!" I announce. "Hey, what's on Scooby's head? Aside from tinsel."

"Reindeer antlers."

"He looks preposterous!" I complain, hands on my waist as I stare down at him.

"He's the dog from The Grinch Who Stole Christmas!" Ellie insists.

"But why?"

"So we can take a cute picture of him in front of the tree once I finish decorating!"

"Don't worry, boy, I'll save you when she isn't looking," I whisper while Scooby barks a sharp reply.

"Everything looks nice," I tell her after sliding the pizza into the oven to bake.

"Thanks! I hope you don't mind that I started without you."

"You're doing a better job than I could have. You have your grandma's eye."

Realizing how tired I am, I grab a beer from the refrigerator, kick off my shoes, and flop down on the couch with a heavy sigh, just like I used to after a long day of investigations.

"Tough day?" Ellie asks.

"Yeah." I could say more, but I wouldn't know where to start. I'm just so frustrated.

"How did the visit with Sammy go?"

"Not great. He admits to closing the bar early, getting drunk, and then going to Ebenita's house to confront her."

"Yikes, did he drive drunk? What did Ebenita say when he showed up at her house?"

"Thankfully, Jack took his keys, so no, he didn't drive himself. I was sure he took a cab, but when I talked to the lawyer, he said he had already thought of that. But none of the cab companies have a record of picking up anyone at the bar and going to Ebenita's house. And no, Sammy doesn't recall seeing her either. He only remembers pounding on the door and yelling, which also squares with what the neighbors witnessed."

"If he didn't drive or take a cab, how did he get there?" Ellie asks.

"It's the craziest thing. He thinks he rode a bike."

"In the snow?"

"Yeah. But he doesn't even own a bike."

"Oh no, did he steal one?" Ellie gasps.

"I don't remember seeing any parked at the bar that night. A bike in a snowstorm would have stood out to me. I think he was too drunk to remember properly. Maybe he hitchhiked?"

"Oh, my gosh! Gramps!" she says excitedly.

"What?"

"There's an e-bike rental station a block from the bar!"

"Those green, motorized bikes people abandon around town?" I ask, taking a gulp of beer. I'm still convinced this is highly unlikely.

"Yes! Well, they aren't just for leaving behind; they're for riding."

"How do those things work, anyway? I've never paid much attention."

"You swipe a credit card at the station or use an app which unlocks the bike. You rent it."

"What do you do with it when you're done?" I'm still confused about how this could work for a drunk Sammy.

"You park it back in the stall."

"Then why do I see them scattered throughout town unattended?"

"Some people leave them at their final stop or when the battery runs out. Then the company uses a tracker to locate the bike, return it to the stall, and charge the battery for the next customer."

"You're telling me you think Sammy rented a bike in a snowstorm and rode over to Ebenita's?"

"It makes sense in a weird way. More sense than him stealing a random bike left out in the snow. Besides, the e-bikes are powered by a small motor, so if a person insists on riding a bike through a snowstorm, that would be the kind to do it with."

"I guess."

"Do you understand where I'm going with this?" she presses.

"Not really."

"You *rent* an e-bike."

Now I feel like an idiot. Some detective I am. "If he rented one, there would be a record of it."

"Yes!" she shouts, throwing her hands up, while Scooby barks excitedly.

"But if he rented a bike and rode it to Ebenita's, where is it now?" As desperate as I am to find answers, this still isn't adding up.

"Wherever else he rode it to. It could still be out there somewhere if the company hasn't picked it up yet."

"I'll take anything I can get at this point," I respond, shaking my head in disbelief.

I dial Greg, but he doesn't answer. Smart man. He's probably at home, actually enjoying his dinner. I leave a message regarding our theory about the e-bike and just as I finish, the pizza is ready.

Ellie eagerly scoots over to a seat at the kitchen table while I pull the pizza from the oven. A rush of warm, aromatic air fills the kitchen, carrying rich scents of golden, bubbling cheese and herbed tomato sauce. The crust is just as I like it, perfectly golden-brown at the edges. I carefully set the pizza on the counter to let it cool for a moment while I lay out plates and napkins.

With a practiced hand (I'm a regular at the pizza joint), I slice it into neat, even wedges, my mouth watering in anticipation. We each take a slice, the cheese stretching into delightful strings as we lift it. Biting into the crust, I savor the perfect combination of crispy and chewy textures, the flavors bursting delightfully in my mouth.

We exchange contented glances and easy banter, putting our troubles aside for the moment while Ellie regales me with tales of customers from the bookstore. Between school work, work at the bookstore, and life in her off-campus apartment, she tells fascinating stories that I never tire of hearing, especially over a delicious meal. I love how the simple act of eating pizza becomes a moment of shared joy and warmth.

After savoring the last bites of dinner, we clear the table, and I relish how my spirits are buoyed by the meal and my granddaughter's company. We place the final touches on the Christmas decorations, with Ellie hanging the remaining ornaments on the tree and me draping one more string of twinkling lights in the front window at Ellie's insistence. Even I enjoy the warm, festive glow the lights cast around the room. We step back to admire our handiwork before Ellie insists we take pictures. Scooby is happy to comply, knowing he'll be rewarded with treats when we're done.

By the time Ellie leaves, the tree is aglow with lights. Scratch that. The entire house is illuminated with lights and Christmas decorations. I may not have planned it, but I must admit it brings back fond memories. At least Scooby is free of his tinsel entanglement, and I promise to hide the reindeer antlers. I'll tell Ellie that Scooby did it after she embarrassed him on social media with all the pictures. After seeing Ellie safely to her car, I lock the front door and make my customary rounds to ensure the remaining doors and windows are secure for the evening.

The quiet of the house settles around me like a cloak while I take in the twinkling tree and the decorations Ellie hung with such care. But now that she's left for the evening, it's back to work. I may have retired from detective work, but the thrill of the chase and the need to put things right is as strong as ever.

I devote the next hour to outlining what I know and charting what we need to investigate further. I rapidly scribble notes, my handwriting scrawling across the pages of an old notebook. It's a familiar comfort. My wife used to tease me when I did this. I often stayed up all night, plotting and planning, arguing that it was times like these when I made a breakthrough. But tonight, any breakthroughs allude me. All I have are more questions, so I'll keep going. Sammy is counting on me, and I'm not about to let my friend down—not at Christmas, not ever.

Chapter 15

I'm pleased, yet not surprised when Greg calls me at 7 a.m.. He's a passionate and dedicated criminal defense lawyer, which is good for Sammy. Our department knew it was crucial to dot every I and cross every T when dealing with him. It drove me bananas at times, but little did I know that one day, I'd be grateful for his commitment to the job.

"I got your message about the e-bike rental, Howie. I'll see what I can dig up, but you know how it is around the holidays," he drawls.

I grumble in agreement. Why am I only now experiencing the frustration of trying to get things done while everyone else winds down for Christmas? Was this always a thing, and I never noticed?

"There's something else," he interrupts my thoughts. I hear him turning pages while he flips through his notes, and I appreciate his thoroughness. "A woman, Mrs. Loretta Kinsley, who owns Whispering Pines Antiquities, an antique shop on the corner of 30th and Pearl Street, just landed on our radar. She and Ebenita clashed repeatedly."

"Over what?" I ask, puzzled. I can only imagine what this woman did to raise Ebenita's ire. Probably very little.

"You may recall the aging storefronts that used to take up that area."

"I do. The antique shop is the only one left."

"Correct. Several years ago, a real estate development company bought up the other shops to make way for a mixed-use development concept."

I scratch my head in wonder. Has it already been several years since that happened? "I remember the drama it caused at the time. Now, most of the store owners have a shop on the ground floor but live on the floors above."

"Yes, that's exactly it."

"Now that you mention it, I recall some controversy about a lone holdout. It was obviously the antique shop."

"Correct again. She was the only owner who refused to sell, so they built around her instead. According to my documentation, Ebenita was one of the most outspoken community members opposing the decision to allow the antique shop to remain. Even long after settling the matter, Ebenita hounded the city council to rethink their decision. She insisted that the shop was a blight on the area and continuously pressured the council to force Ms. Kinsley to sell it to the developers."

"Ebenita was obsessed with driving this woman out because she didn't like how her shop looked compared to the newer buildings? She wanted someone's shop torn down because she thought it was ugly?"

"That's what it sounds like," Greg says.

"I know I'm not supposed to speak ill of the dead, but Ebenita was a piece of work."

"That she was."

I know the shop he's referring to, and I'd hardly call it ugly. It's an older shop, and yes, it looks out of place next to the sleek, modern buildings, but I wouldn't call it a blight. Personally, I miss the old Boulder. It was charming and traditional. I still love strolling through historic neighborhoods like mine, especially in the spring when the trees are blossoming and the tulips peek through the warming soil.

Greg continues. "According to my paperwork, last summer, Ebenita and Loretta were involved in an altercation on the Pearl Street Mall where they were both ticketed for disturbing the peace and disorderly conduct."

"Is Loretta a violent person?" I ask, trying to picture the older ladies slugging it out in the middle of the mall.

"Oh, that's just the beginning." Greg sighs. "According to police records, Loretta also sent threatening emails to Ebenita."

"And with Ebenita gone, Loretta's problems disappear," I point out. "I take it you want me to interview her?"

"Yes. I find that talking to people in person is better than relying solely on paperwork and police records."

"I agree. Scooby and I will head over there now." Scooby's ears tilt forward the moment I say that, making that familiar dachshund triangle look. He's also developed a sixth sense about when I'm even considering a walk. When I nod at him, he scurries down his ramp, sprinting for the front door.

Wearing my usual plaid shirt and corduroys, I bundle up before we brave the chilly winter air. Loretta Kinsley's shop is a relic in itself, not unlike Jasper's locksmith store. It sits in front of a vegan bakery and a sleek tech store. The windows are dressed with garlands and red ribbons, while the display items speak of times long past.

The bell above the door jingles, announcing my presence. Every surface is covered by objects that hold their own stories. Mrs. Kinsley is a stern-looking woman whose sharp eyes appraise me. She's not exactly petite. It's possible she's strong enough to strangle Ebenita. As I expected, however, her face softens as soon as she sees Scooby. It's impossible not to appreciate a wiener dog! Hopefully this encourages her to talk to me honestly.

"Good morning, Mrs. Kinsley. My name is Howard O'Sullivan, and I was hoping to have a word with you?" I start. "It's about Ebenita Scroogina."

"Are you as glad as I am that she's dead?" she asks curtly while leading me to a corner of the shop that serves as her office—one cluttered with papers and even more antiques to line the walls.

"That's a loaded question," I admit. "I'm aware of your dispute with her."

"And I yours," she comments briskly. Interesting. I didn't realize my story had reached beyond the walls of the Veteran's Hearth. "That woman wanted to tear down my history, my family's legacy, because she doesn't like how my shop looks next to the new development. But this shop is my life. My grandparents started it, you know."

"Did you ever think of... getting rid of the problem?" I ask carefully.

Her gaze doesn't waver. "If you're asking whether I killed her, Mr. O'Sullivan, the answer is no."

"What happened last summer when you and Ebenita were on the Pearl Street Mall?"

Her eyes narrow as she contemplates how much of her story she should share. "I saw Ebenita walking in my direction, and to avoid a public confrontation, I crossed to the other side of the mall. I hope you know *she's* the one who followed me. *She* confronted me."

"So you two argued. Is that it?"

"No, not exactly."

I lean forward in my chair, resting my hands on my knees. "Then what, exactly?" I push.

"We argued, and it got heated. Heated enough that shoppers stopped to watch. Then, out of the blue, she hauled off and walloped me with her purse!"

"What did you do after that?"

"I hit her back," she admits.

"With?"

"*My* purse."

"Did it escalate from there?"

"No. One of the police officers who patrols the mall saw us, so he gave us a stern warning and a ticket. It only got worse because several people filmed the confrontation, posting it on social media. I was hoping the judge would dismiss the ticket, and I think he would have if one of the videos hadn't gone viral. People were warning their friends Boulder is out of control and they should stay away. He said we should be ashamed of ourselves and that he expected that type of behavior from teenagers, not older women. It was humiliating, and I should have just walked away without saying a word instead of letting Ebenita suck me into a mess."

"I'm also told you emailed threats to Ebenita."

"Yes, I did." She hangs her head. "I know how this must look, but I swear I'm not normally like this. That woman just brought out the worst in me. I threatened her — in writing — and yes, I once lost my temper with her, but actual murder? That's not something I could do."

"Could you tell me where you were at midnight the night she was murdered?"

Loretta laughs. "You seriously want an alibi from me?"

"If you don't mind, it could be helpful."

"I was at home. Asleep. Like I am every night at midnight."

"Can anyone vouch for you?"

"Of course not. I live alone! Is that a problem?"

"I'm just trying to get the facts straight."

"I swear to you, I didn't murder Ebenita, but I wouldn't mind shaking hands with the person who did." She hardens upon seeing my expression. "Yes, it sounds awful, but that woman caused me so much distress I requested a prescription for anti-anxiety medication. I know how this must look. Now that Ebenita's gone, I won't have to contend with her pressuring city officials to force me off my property. I'll do just about anything to stay here, but I draw the line at murder."

Realizing I won't get anything more from Loretta at this time, I thank her for our conversation, but just as I start to leave the shop, I notice a pair of dirty boots by the front door that look out of place. They're definitely not antique. I desperately want to pick them up to check the tread, but I don't want to tip my hand. I glance back, and Loretta isn't looking, so I quickly pull out my phone and snap a picture, but when I look back again, she's staring at me with a perplexed gaze.

Did she see me? That was careless. She'll dispose of the shoes if she thinks I'm onto her. I point out a clock in the window display. "I think my grandparents had one of those!" I insist. She smiles but doesn't say anything. Darnit. She knows I'm up to something.

Ultimately, I leave, experiencing a chill not just from the cold weather but from the dead ends I keep hitting. I'm struggling not to let this case get too personal for me. More personal than it already is, anyway.

As a cop, I went out of my way to keep things strictly professional. I learned early on that taking cases personally was the surest way to burn out in law enforcement. And believe me, there were a lot of cases I could have easily gotten in trouble with. A young girl would go missing or end up dead, and I couldn't help but think about what I would do if that were my daughter or granddaughter. Whenever a woman was assaulted, in the darkest recesses of my mind, I would admit that if someone ever did that to my wife, you'd have to physically lock me up to prevent me from enforcing my own kind of payback.

It's best for Sammy that I *not* take this personally, at least not too personally. He needs my practiced eye and not my emotional eye. But it's extra hard on this one to maintain a professional distance. I must be as objective as I can here. It's what's best for Sammy.

Scooby and I barely get in the front door when Greg calls again. Please, please, please, have good news, I mutter before pressing accept.

"I have what may or may not be good news," he says.

"Lay it on me," I tell him while kneeling down to pull off Scooby's coat.

"There's a record of Sammy renting a bike on the night in question."

"Well, I'll be darned." He *must* have been drunk if he rode a bike in the snow.

"He checked it out at 10:37 p.m."

"That's not good," I groan. "The prosecution will claim it gave him ample time to go to Ebenita's and kill her at midnight. That easily places him at her house at 11 p.m.

like Irene Jensen told me. My granddaughter said they track them with a chip. What time did he check it back in?"

"He didn't."

"Then where's the bike?" This whole idea of being able to rent a bike only to drop it wherever you want, still perplexes me.

"I'm not sure."

"Can they track it down?"

"Yes, but—"

"--let me guess. It will take time."

"Unfortunately, yes."

"Okay. By the way, I talked to Ms. Kinsley, and she admits to getting in a fight with Ebenita and threatening her."

"Alibi?" Greg asks.

"She claims she was home in bed but has no one to corroborate that."

"Stay on it."

"Of course."

After hanging up with Greg, once again, I find myself at my desk, pieces of the case spread before me. We have suspects with motives, a timeline muddled with inconsistencies, and now, a potential and problematic link to the rented e-bike.

And it all hinges on time — something that's moving as sluggishly as molasses all because it's less than a week before Christmas. There's a killer somewhere in this tangled web of clues and dead ends. But where?

Chapter 16

I still need to see Alastair McClellan, the artisan steel worker, but for the moment, finding the bike is a priority. It could be a crucial piece to clearing Sammy. I realize it's just a hunch, and if I admitted it to anyone else, they might laugh at me, but my instincts seldom lead me astray. and it's been nagging at me. If he didn't use the bike to return, how *did* he get home?

As preposterous as it sounds that he took a bike out in the cold and snow, it's crazier still to think that he walked back to the bar. Yet none of the cab companies have a record of picking him up. I just don't get it. I'm missing something, but what?

After promising a disgruntled Scooby I'd make it up to him for leaving him at home, I drive to Ebenita's neighborhood where I park a block away to avoid unwanted attention. If we don't find the bike, the prosecutor could say Sammy must have disposed of it to cover his tracks?

I would argue it was too cold, and he was too drunk to think that far ahead, but I'm not sure that would convince a jury. If he had spent that much time outside that night, surely he would have suffered from frostbite or possibly worse. Plus, he didn't kill Ebenita, so there would be no need to dispose of the bike in the first place. But again, I'm not sure that would persuade a jury.

After circling the block on foot, failing to discover it haphazardly propped against a tree in someone's yard as I had hoped, I then make my way to Ebenita's place. I don't remember seeing a bike at her house, but I wasn't looking for one. If only I had known that they'd accuse Sammy of her murder, there are so many things I would have done differently that night. Soon, Ebenita's house looms ahead, its windows darker and more uninviting than ever. The snow crunches unnaturally loud beneath my feet. I don't want anyone to see me lurking and call Detective Rodriguez.

I approach the backyard, my movements cautious and calculated. The fence is old and wooden and creaks slightly when I test its sturdiness before hoisting myself up. I don't think to question whether I should be climbing fences at my age before swinging my leg over the top. Landing softly on the other side, I'm grateful I didn't break anything - on the fence or my aging bones. I crouch low while sneaking through Ebenita's backyard, but there's no sign of the bike.

There's no sign of watchful neighbors either, thankfully. I'm disappointed to discover, after crossing the yard, there's no bike. However, instead of hopping the fence again, I use the gate to let myself out. Just as I congratulate myself for getting through the backyard undetected, a familiar car pulls up. Detective Rodriguez steps out, wearing the sternest of expressions. Does she have a tracking chip on me that I don't know about?

"Howie, what are you doing here?" she demands, her voice betraying her frustration.

"I'm just trying to help, Detective," I respond, locking eyes with her.

"By sneaking around and potentially contaminating evidence?" she claps back. "We've discussed this before. You know you shouldn't be here."

"But we're after the same thing," I point out.

"And what's that?"

"Justice."

She sighs, her stance softening just a bit. "I get it. But you have to let us do our job."

I take a deep breath, knowing what I'm about to say walks a fine line between helping and hurting my friend. I'm confessing in the hopes it will foster some semblance of partnership. "Sammy rented an e-bike that we believe he rode here on the night in question."

She raises her eyebrows, a mix of surprise and interest coloring her expression. "That's unexpected news. But I appreciate you sharing. Sammy's lawyer tracked that down?"

I shift uncomfortably. I know she'd learn of it eventually anyway, and I'm hoping that by sharing my news, she'll be more apt to share something, too. "More or less." I don't need to disclose every little bit after all.

"Do we have a timeline?" she presses.

"He rented it at 10:37 p.m.," I admit reluctantly.

"So he had plenty of time to ride the bike here and murder Ebenita at midnight," she muses.

"*If* he was the killer, which he isn't."

"Wait a minute," she says after rolling her eyes at my insistence that Sammy is innocent. "Is that what you were doing in the backyard? Is the bike there?" she asks, peering around me at the gate I just exited.

"It isn't," I explain.

"Are you sure?" she crooks her head at me as if she's wondering whether she can trust me on this.

"I have no reason to lie to you," I tell her before remembering the key still sitting uncomfortably in my pocket. "If the bike were there, you'd find it eventually anyway."

"So your theory is he rented an e-bike and rode it over here but then did what with it? I don't recall my officers finding an e-bike at the bar or Mr. Thompson's home. You do know they can track those, right?"

"Yes, but we're still waiting on the information."

Her professional instincts clearly piqued, Detective Rodriguez jots down some notes. "Have you searched the community center for it?"

"No, actually, I haven't." Because I knew Sammy was at Ebenita's that night, her house was my first thought. I didn't consider the community center because he was never there. Not with Ebenita, anyway. No matter what Detective Rodriguez thinks.

"Want to take a ride with me?" she suggests.

"I can do that." If we don't find the bike there, which I'm sure we won't, perhaps it will persuade Detective Rodriguez to look at other suspects. It's worth a shot, at least.

"We could have just walked, you know," I remind her as we get in her car.

"I know, but it's cold out," she complains.

"Your car *is* nice and toasty." The heater in my Chevy pickup hasn't been working as well as I'd like, but I've been procrastinating taking it into the shop. Not that I can't afford it, I just don't want them to remind me it's probably time I considered a new one.

"How is retirement treating you?" she asks in what I recognize as an apparent attempt to lead the topic away from the case - at least momentarily.

"You mean until Baxter, Sterling & Dunn hired me to investigate this case?"

"Yes, that's what I mean," she chuckles.

"It's okay. Maybe even a little boring, if I'm being honest. Don't get me wrong, at my age, I don't need to be chasing bad guys down dark alleys—"

"--or hopping fences?" she interrupts.

"Yeah, I shouldn't be doing that either," I admit.

"You're not *that* old," she insists.

"Most of the time, I don't feel it. Plus, Scooby keeps me active. My granddaughter does, too," I add.

"Where *is* your constant canine companion, by the way?" she asks.

"I made him stay home this time."

"Didn't think he could jump a fence?"

"Okay, I admit it." I throw my hands in the air. "I jumped the fence. Although, now I realize I could have just used the gate. How about you?" I ask. "How do you like working for the Boulder Police Department?"

"It's been an interesting journey so far. There are obvious challenges, of course. Even though I'm not a new detective, I am a newbie in the department, and I'm a woman, so that comes with its own issues. But honestly, I'm happy with it. I made the right move." She turns to me with a genuine smile.

"I hope they don't hassle you too much as a woman. Back in my day, female detectives and officers were few and far between. I feel bad for the ones who had to blaze the way for the rest of you and were treated poorly. I never engaged in any of that, for the record - my lovely wife would have killed me... They aren't making life too hard, are they? Because I could talk to them if you want."

"Oh, no, I'm not complaining or anything. And believe me, I know how hard it was for the previous generation. It's just the usual – being second-guessed, and sometimes I'm overlooked when they don't even realize they're doing it. But I've learned to navigate it pretty well. I find it works best when I can prove my worth beyond any doubt, prove that I'm capable."

"I've seen your work, and you're far more than capable. Don't let anyone's doubts hold you back. Including your own. You've got a sharp mind for this job – Boulder PD's lucky to have you."

"Thanks, Howie. I really appreciate that. You have a stellar reputation in the department."

Just as we pull into the community center's parking lot, I realize now's my chance to ask the question that's been nagging at me. "Hey, something is bugging me about this case."

"Go ahead," she responds.

"What's Sammy's motive for killing Ebenita? I mean, aside from her just being an incredibly disagreeable person."

She crooks her head. "He hasn't told you about their past?"

"No. What about it? What past?"

"You should ask him."

Before I can press her for more details, she puts the car in park and gets out. I've already talked to Sammy; he swore he told me everything he knows. What could she have on him that *I* don't know about?

We agree to split up to maximize our search for the elusive bike. Once we're done here, I'll insist she tell me what she knows. Detective Rodriguez heads around the corner while I make a beeline to the trash dumpsters. I've been to numerous crime scenes where the perp either threw evidence out or hid it behind the dumpsters hoping it would never be found.

I'm sure if the bike had been here all along, they would have found it in their initial search, but it never hurts to double-check. Even though I'm convinced this search will be fruitless, we must be thorough. When I approach the dumpsters, however, my heart sinks upon spotting the distinctive frame of an e-bike tucked behind the steel structures.

"Rodriguez, over here!" I call out, my voice tinged with disappointment.

She jogs over to the dumpsters, her expression hardening when she sees the bike.

"We don't know that this is the bike Sammy used," I quickly protest, even though I know it's too much of a coincidence. It's not like it's the middle of spring when bikes are often scattered around town.

"This is it," she says with a grim certainty. "This is the bike Sammy rode here, and when he realized it could implicate him, he stashed it behind the dumpsters, hoping no one would find it. Perhaps he intended to come back later to permanently dispose of it."

Before I can register another weak protest, the team she had already called in earlier to help search, begins processing the scene and examining the bike for additional evidence. As officers surround our location, I experience a stabbing pang of regret. She would have discovered this eventually, but why can't I shake a feeling of betrayal? Because of me, we've unearthed evidence that seems to solidify Sammy's guilt, despite my gut still telling me there's more to the story. I stand aside helplessly, watching the scene unfold, still wrestling with my conscience.

"I can have one of the officers drive you back to your truck," Detective Rodriguez interrupts my thoughts.

"Nah, that's okay. I can walk."

"Are you sure? It's freezing out."

"It's not that far. And I need the walk to help me think."

"Howie, for what it's worth, I'm sorry this looks so bad for your friend."

"I hear you, Detective, but no matter how things appear, I know Sammy; he's innocent, and I'll do whatever it takes to prove it." It isn't until I get back to my truck that I remember I never got to press her on Sammy's motive.

Chapter 17

Gripping the cold steering wheel, and cursing when the heater still won't work like I want it to, I leave Ebenita's neighborhood, passing the community center as I go. I admit it, I miss the powerful heater in Detective Rodriguez car.

I drive a 30-year-old, once black, now faded to a dark gray, cassette tape only, Chevy C1500 pickup with 183,000 miles on it. Lisa constantly nagged me to get a new truck. But I like this one; it's a time capsule on wheels filled with memories of road trips, family outings, and years of dependable service. This truck, is a symbol of resilience and enduring reliability. Qualities I appreciate in both life and machinery. But I sure wish the heater worked better.

The police continue to swarm around the dumpsters where we found the e-bike, while the same questions plague me. How did it end up there? How did Sammy get home without it? And what does Detective Rodriguez know, or *think* she knows, that I don't?

The streets pass by in a blur as I mull over her words. What could this secret motive be? And why didn't Sammy tell me when I visited him at lockup? What's he hiding? I asked him point blank if he had anything else to share, and he reassured me he didn't. Why would my friend lie to me? He knows I'm on his side. I flip on the windshield wipers when the sky starts to spit snow again, mesmerized by how they rhythmically cut across the windshield, mirroring the back and forth of my thoughts.

As I pull into the garage, I take comfort in knowing that Scooby will be there to greet me enthusiastically despite my having left him at home earlier. All will be forgiven, and he'll think of me as his best friend again. Plus, I'll give him a treat for being a good boy.

Since adopting him, I've been pleasantly surprised by the joy and companionship he's brought me. I'm almost embarrassed to admit I wasn't sure at first if I wanted the responsibility that comes with a dog. Still, I've happily embraced the routine of walks and playtime, finding unexpected peace in these simple activities.

His over-the-top greetings, even when I'm gone less than a minute to take the trash out, and his unwavering loyalty fill my home with a warmth I didn't even realize I was missing. His keen senses and alertness also add an element of security. A trait I appreciate, of course. Most of all, I cherish the quiet moments of connection. Scooby's companionship has brought a comforting, lively spirit to my now too-quiet life, and I don't know what I'd do without him.

As I predicted, my canine sidekick greets me at the door, wagging his tail vigorously while blissfully unaware of the turmoil in my mind. I scratch his ears and ask him if he wants a treat. Of course, he wants a treat, he tells me. Or at least he would if he could talk.

When I select a treat from his special jar in the cupboard, I realize the gnawing in my stomach isn't just anxiety – I'm hungry. It's past lunchtime, so I should eat before I do any more sleuthing. It never helps to work on an empty stomach.

A sandwich will do. Nothing fancy. Just some ham and cheese on rye bread. For good measure, I add a slice of tomato and a leaf of lettuce. I'm relieved to discover I have potato chips in the cupboard. A sandwich without potato chips is practically inedible. I throw in a Dos Equis Lager while I'm at it. Hey, it's a perk of being retired. If I want a beer with lunch, I'll have one.

I turn on the the afternoon news, mostly for background noise. Sometimes the house is just too quiet. I ignore the commercial for toothpaste but when the news returns and the headline on the screen show the reporter is interviewing Marc Whitfield a member of city council, I take notice.

"I'm here with Councilman Marc Whitfield of the Boulder City Council to talk about a cause which is near and dear to him, the Snowy Wishes Toy Drive."

"Thank you Carlie. I'd like to thank everyone who donated so far. We really appreciate the support and your viewers should know it's not too late. If you still want to donate you can, but you have to hurry down to City Hall because the deadline is today."

"What prompted you to support the toy drive?"

"Well, Carlie, I want your viewers to know I'm not just a politician. I'm here to serve the community. Did you know that as a child, I once spent Christmas Day in the hospital?"

"No, I didn't know that."

"That's why I support the program, in addition to strengthening my ties to my beloved community, showcasing my commitment to the welfare of this city's most vulnerable residents..."

After that I tune out as I scribble down the name of the city councilman. If he's involved with the Snowy Wishes Toy Drive, surely he'd be willing to help us with locating a new venue for Pedals of Promise.

"Okay, Scoobs, back to work," I announce after sliding my plate into the dishwasher and tossing my empty beer bottle into the recycle bin. I sit at my desk, ready to plot my next moves. The key in my pocket reminds me of one more thing needing follow up.

I don't think just driving out to Alastair McClellan's shop unannounced is the best idea. My experience with people who are wary of strangers and purposely living off the grid is they don't like surprises, which I understand. Unless it's my granddaughter or a close friend, I don't care for folks showing up at *my* door unannounced, either.

I dial the number Jasper gave me and I'm not surprised when there's no answer, so I leave a detailed message about wanting to meet and discuss the key I found near Ebenita's body. I hang up, feeling like I just made a teeny bit of progress, yet there's still a growing list of unanswered questions.

On a whim, I decide to try searching public records. My fingers fly across the keyboard as I type in the search parameters. Mr. Kowalski and Mr. Bennett mentioned Ebenita threatened to sue Bennett, but neither said whether she did so successfully.

Given that money is often a factor in homicides, it would be helpful to know if Ebenita was successful. When the search results load, I'm not surprised to see that a jury awarded Ebenita $15,000 in her case against Larry Bennett.

"$15,000 worth of motive," I mutter, making a note of it on the paper next to my computer. I wonder if Greg has seen this. But before I email him the results of my search, I pause. I'm still in the records portal. What if?

No. Absolutely not. No way Sammy did anything to Ebenita as serious as Detective Rodriguez implied. I can't believe I'm doing this, but I'll just make a quick search, and I'll feel better when I come up with nothing. There's no way Sammy lied to me or held back something as vital as the detective hinted. But at least this way, I can confirm it.

Yet, when the search results load, my heart skips a beat. There it is, clear as day – an assault charge against Sammy and a restraining order filed by Ebenita two years ago. How is this possible? My mind races, piecing together a narrative I refuse to consider because it paints such a dark picture. No way Sammy assaulted someone. No way Sammy assaulted a woman, for sure. I'm dismayed to see there are no details included in the record—just the charges.

I need to see Sammy right away. However, my phone rings before I can double-check the prison visiting hours. It's Toby the warehouse owner. I hadn't told him about the cancellation because I hoped I wouldn't have to. I was still wishing for a Christmas miracle moment - like in those Hallmark Christmas movies, my wife loved so much. While I teased her about the cookie-cutter plots and absurdly cheesy storylines, even I was sometimes moved by the uplifting endings and had to excuse myself a time or two when they made me tear up. What I wouldn't give to be able to complain about her Christmas movie marathons again.

And, as the great philosopher Bart Simpson claimed in their first episode, if there's anything TV taught him, miracles happen to kids at Christmas. I know, I know, I'm not a kid, and this isn't a Hallmark movie or a cartoon, but a guy can dream.

"Hey there Toby."

"Hi Howie, I just overheard some disturbing news. Is it true?"

"You heard Ebenita Scroogina convinced the city council to cancel the Pedals of Promise event."

"So it *is* true."

"I'm afraid so."

"And given that I agreed to store 30 bikes for free because you promised me they'd be gone on Christmas Day, don't you think you should have told me?"

"You know what Toby? Yes, I should have told you. Honestly, I hoped to come up with an alternative before

I had to call you about it. But that's all on me, and I apologize for not being upfront with you."

"Okay, well, I appreciate the apology, but I still need the bikes removed before the 26th."

"I know this is a big ask, given everything I just told you, but is there any way we could have one extra day?"

"I wish I could, but they're coming on the 26th to tear the warehouse down, and any delay costs me $10,000 a day. So unless you have $10,000 to pay for an extra day, I can't."

"Can't say that I do."

"I'm sorry, but I can't give you an extension."

"I appreciate your patience."

"Let me know as soon as possible if you come up with a solution."

"Sure thing."

Can this day get any better?

Chapter 18

Admitting it would help to bounce ideas off someone I can trust, I text Jack.

I need your help. Are you free?

U @ home

Yes

BRT

I assume that means Jack is on his way, and sure enough, twenty minutes later, when he pulls up to my house, I have to explain to a supremely annoyed Scooby that he must sit this one out. While having Scooby with me is usually a benefit, sometimes, toting a dog with me is a hindrance. When he realizes even his most pathetic, woe-as-me expression isn't enough to talk me out of leaving him at home, he pouts before marching off to one of his beds in the corner. (Yes, he has multiple beds, if you can believe it.)

"I'm so sorry, Scoobs," I tell him again before shutting the door behind me. I'll make it up to him tomorrow with an extra long walk.

When I climb into Jack's car with a big sigh, he turns to me concerned.

"You sound stressed."

"I have about 4000 things on my plate right now, and I need help."

"Anything you need."

"Where do I start?" I ask, feeling more burdened than I realized.

"Anywhere."

"I just got off the phone with Toby."

"The guy who's storing the bikes for us?"

"Yes, that's him."

"Uh oh. I take it we still have to get them out of the warehouse by Christmas Day?"

"Yes. And I don't blame the guy. He's been more than patient with us. Considering he wasn't the one who agreed to hold them in the first place, it was generous of him to continue doing it. Unfortunately, the contractors hired to tear down the warehouse are scheduled to start on the 26th, and if he postpones, there's a $10,000 penalty. Per day!"

Jack whistles softly. "That's steep."

"He explained earlier that bringing in all the construction equipment and labor is costly, and understandably, they don't appreciate delays."

"Time is money." Jack grimaces. "So we have 30 bikes, which were supposed to go out on the 25th—"

"--don't forget about the big dinner that the restaurants and volunteers have already promised and that the families are counting on."

"Oh, man, I forgot that part," Jack says, smacking his forehead. "Plus all the food and supplies they inevitably ordered well in advance."

"Yeah, Ebenita really inconvenienced a lot of people with her shenanigans."

"That's putting it mildly. What's our next step?" he asks.

"While eating lunch, I saw a guy from the city council on TV. Marc Whitfield is his name. A reporter interviewed him about the Snowy Wishes Toy Drive."

"I've heard of that. It's a program that donates toys to kids in hospitals, right?"

"Yeah, he's the chairman of the committee or something like that. He told her they've collected 265 toys, which they'll start passing out tomorrow. But they're still accepting donations at City Hall today. Assuming he's still there, I want to talk to him in person."

"Do you think he could get our event permit reinstated?" Jack grips the steering wheel in anticipation.

"That would be my first choice. Although luck hasn't been on our side lately."

"Good point."

"If he can't do that, perhaps he could pull some strings and get us a new venue," I explain as Jack nods, steering the car towards City Hall.

I won't tell Jack what I learned about Sammy and Ebenita just yet. I want us to focus on the councilman for now. It's easy to find Councilman Whitfield's office, which, as I saw on the news, is buzzing with excitement. Volunteers move from pile to pile of brightly colored toys and stacks of gift-wrapped boxes. The hallway is filled with the chatter of coordinating efforts and the rustle of wrapping paper while each toy finds its place in a carefully labeled bin.

"Excuse me, where can I find Councilman Whitfield?" I ask a harried volunteer.

"In his office, I think," the volunteer points through a doorway seconds before someone bumps into her, knocking tape and a roll of glittering green wrapping paper from her hands. "It's a bit crazy here," she apologizes to us.

"That's okay, I'll show myself in," I tell her. The councilman's office is just as busy as the hallway, with volunteers crisscrossing the room, trying to avoid stepping on each other.

"You guys! Be careful about things in this office!" a woman in a suit says as she bends down to retrieve a file from the floor which appears to have been stepped on several times already.

"Volunteers?" she asks us in an exasperated tone while rescuing a vase someone else nearly knocks to the ground.

"No. I'm sorry, we're just here to see the Councilman," I explain.

"He's in there," she points to another room right before a stack of carefully placed toys comes crashing down. "I said be careful!" she shouts, hurrying for the pile.

Jack and I move toward the office, where we find the Councilman behind his desk signing documents. He's so busy he doesn't realize we're there at first.

"Excuse me, Councilman, I'm Howie O'Sullivan and this is Jack Marshall and we run the Pedals of Promise event."

Whitfield is a middle-aged man with a friendly demeanor, but his face falls slightly when I mention the event.

"Ah, yes..." he says, putting down his pen and folding his hands.

"I can see you're busy here, so I'll get right to the point. We're in a tough place with the event permit being canceled. I also understand this could sound indelicate, given what's happened, but could you approve a new permit for us at the Starlight Community Center?"

"I truly wish I could help, fellas, but I'm sure you know how it is with bureaucratic red tape. Once a permit is rescinded, city code dictates you restart the permit process, which takes at least 30 days," he informs us with genuine regret.

"Okay. I'm not surprised," I tell him. "I'll take another stab at this. Any chance you know of a place that would be available to host the event?" I press.

He looks pained. "I'd be shocked to find a venue that isn't already booked this time of year, but I'll tell you what. I'll see what I can do. Maybe there's a space with a last-minute cancellation. You could make use of their permit too," he offers helpfully.

"We really appreciate that," I tell him.

"Sorry our trip didn't work out," Jack says as we head back to his car.

"I would have been shocked if it worked, but I wanted to at least get on his radar, given his involvement with the toy drive. I felt like showing up in person might make it seem more real to him. But now I regret not meeting with him beforehand. Perhaps he could have lobbied the rest of the city council to vote against Ebenita."

"But who could have guessed that Ebenita would succeed in getting this canceled at the last minute? I bet even she was surprised she pulled it off."

"Hey, here's a crazy idea," he interjects. "Let's try the Holiday Inn on 28th Street. They have weddings and big parties there all the time. Like you said, let's show up in person. Maybe they'll feel sorry for us."

"Because you're in a wheelchair?" I ask, shocked he would suggest this.

"No, because you're an old man."

When I laugh for the first time in a while, I appreciate how good it feels.

On our way to the Holiday Inn, Jack glances over at me. "Anything else on your mind?" he asks. "Aside from the obvious, of course."

"I found something," I say, breaking my silence. "According to the public records I was researching, Sammy was once accused of assaulting Ebenita."

Jack's eyebrows shoot up in surprise. "Sammy? No way. Not a chance."

"I agree," I tell him, a knot twisting in my stomach. "But earlier, when I asked Detective Rodriguez about a motive, she said I should talk to Sammy about his past with Ebenita. That's why I decided to check out the public records on a lark, convinced I wouldn't find anything but, much to my shock, I did. Right there in black and white. Sammy assaulted Ebenita, and she got a restraining order against him."

"Hmmm, Detective Rodriguez didn't elaborate?"

"Nope. And we didn't have a chance to talk about it again."

"What did Greg say about it? He must know."

"I haven't asked him. I kind of want to talk to Sammy about it in person. Before, when I visited him in lockup, he swore he couldn't think of anything that would give Detective Rodriguez reason to think he had motive. And yet, when I saw it in the public records search, I felt like he lied to me. Even though I know there's no way he assaulted Ebenita."

"That's a pretty big thing to forget about," Jack says.

"Exactly. So, he lied? Why not just tell me? He had to have known it would come out eventually."

"And visiting hours are done for the day, but I think we should see Sammy together tomorrow and ask him about it," Jack insists, pulling into the hotel parking lot.

I'm not surprised, unfortunately, when the manager dashes our hopes. "I'm sorry, we're completely booked through January," she tells us with an apologetic smile.

"If you get a cancellation, let us know," Jack tells her.

"Oh, I know, what about that big church on Mapleton Avenue," I suggest. But the story is the same. "We'd love to help, but there's just no space left," the church coordinator informs us, her hands clasped to her chest in regret.

"Seems like we're out of luck on *all* fronts today," Jack says on our way back to his car.

"I think we've been out of luck for a while," I reply, struggling under the weight of our unsuccessful day. "Hey, while we're out, can we make one last stop?" I ask.

"Sure, where?"

"Patty's Pot Emporium down the street."

"You want to get some weed?" he asks, surprised.

"No, I want to double-check on the neighbor's alibi."

"Whose what where?" he laughs. "There's a neighbor with an alibi?"

"I guess that did seem out of the blue," I admit. "Ebenita successfully sued her next-door neighbor Larry Bennett for $15,000."

"Ouch!"

"Yeah. When I questioned him about his alibi and whether he saw or heard anything the night Ebenita was murdered, he told me he's a night shift security guard at the pot store and didn't get home until 12:30 in the morning."

"Do you think he's a suspect?"

"With Ebenita gone, that $15,000 award goes away. That's a lot of motive," I insist.

"$15,000 worth of motive." Jack emphasizes.

We pull into the parking lot of the pot shop and I'm curious. I've never been to one before, so I don't know what to expect. I imagine a disorganized bohemian vibe with earthy tones, and mismatched ambient lighting, topped off by smoky air where we run the risk of a contact high. Will we find someone sober enough to answer our questions?

But the store is nothing like I expected. The lobby is bare except for a few colorful signs advertising this month's specials along with a man with gray hair pulled back in a ponytail, wearing a Vietnam Veterans cap, sitting on a stool behind a computer monitor. There's no smoke and it doesn't smell like pot. At all. I can see the store through a doorway, behind the man and it's quite organized.

"Good afternoon, gentlemen; how can I help you?"

"Hi there, I'm Howard O'Sullivan, and this is Jack Marshall."

"You fellas veterans?"

"Yes."

"Thank you for your service," he says, standing up to shake our hands.

"Thank you," we tell him.

"I'm hoping you can answer a question for us," I get right to the point. Can you tell us if Larry Bennett was working on Tuesday night?"

"Bennett?" he laughs, then looks around to make sure no one is listening. "He hasn't worked here in over a month."

"Are you sure?"

"Sure as I'm sitting here today. When they fired him, it took a half dozen cops to escort him out."

"Why? What did he do?"

The man leans in close and whispers. "They say he stole $15,000."

Chapter 19

Jack and I step out of the pot shop, the bell on the door jingling softly behind us. I honestly thought that confirming the neighbor's alibi was a mere formality. Even though I wasn't convinced Patty's Pot Emporium would answer my questions. When I was on the job, some places happily accommodated us, while others pretty much kicked us to the curb. Today, after what seemed like unsurmountable struggles, we finally stumbled upon a bit of luck coming across another veteran.

As we make our way back to Jack's car, the clerk's shocking revelation and its implications hang heavily between us. Not only did Bennett lie about where he was the night Ebenita was murdered, he was fired for allegedly stealing the exact amount she won from him in the lawsuit. It's all way too much to be a coincidence.

"Could this be enough to get Sammy released?" Jack asks, clicking his seatbelt in place and starting the car.

"With what we know at the moment? I don't think so. But it definitely warrants a conversation with Detective Rodriguez."

"So what do we do next?" Jack asks.

"Good question. You hungry?"

"Famished! I really miss the Veteran's Hearth."

"Me too." I sigh.

"Pizza?" he suggests.

"I had pizza this week, so yeah, it's time again."

Jack chuckles, turning the car around at the next corner to make his way to the pizza restaurant. I don't have to ask which one. His favorite is Pizzazzle's Pie Parlor.

"I have plenty of beer in the refrigerator, too, in case you were wondering."

"I never doubted you," he says.

As we make our way to Pizzazzle's, the conversation shifts back and forth while we consider our next move. The facts are starting to stack up, but not in a way that gives us concrete answers. There's still something missing, a piece of the puzzle we're not seeing.

But just as we arrive at Pizzazzle's, my phone rings, interrupting our conversation. Even though I don't recognize the number, I answer, hoping it's Councilman Whitfield's office. Maybe they found a place for our event!

"Mr. O'Sullivan?" an elderly woman's voice comes across the connection.

"Yes."

"It's Irene Jensen, the woman who lives next to Ebenita. We met the other day. You had your adorable dog with you."

"Yes, of course; what can I do for you?" I ask.

"There's someone in Ebenita's house," she says, her voice dropping to a whisper. She sounds fearful.

"It's probably just the police still investigating." I try to reassure her.

"But would the police break a window to get in?" she asks causing me a surge of alarm.

"No, Irene, that's not right. Hang up and call 911 right now," I urge her.

"Then lock your doors and don't let anyone in until you know it's the police."

"Okay." Her voice trembles.

"You'll be fine; just do what I said," I tell her when she doesn't hang up immediately.

"I'll do it now," she assures me, and the phone goes silent.

"What on earth was that about?" Jack asks.

"That was Irene Jensen. Ebenita's next-door neighbor. She's the one who told me she saw Sammy at Ebenita's at 11:00 the night Ebenita was murdered."

"Good gravy, someone is breaking into her house? Why is she calling you?"

"Not Irene's house. Ebenita's house."

"Is she sure?"

"She said someone broke a window."

"That doesn't sound good." Jack worries.

"It could be kids causing trouble, or maybe a homeless person seeking shelter from the bitter cold," I speculate.

"But..." Jack trails off.

"What if it's Bennett the neighbor on the other side?" I suggest. "Knowing her house is vacant, he could be looking for cash or valuables to sell."

"He's unemployed, after all. And according to Patty's Pot Emporium, he isn't above stealing," Jack adds.

"Or, he could be looking to destroy evidence that points to him as the killer."

"We should check it out," Jack says, decisively. "Assuming the police are already on their way, of course."

"I agree."

He deftly throws the car in reverse, backing out of the parking spot, thoughts of pizza forgotten. Although not entirely. Who forgets about pizza entirely?

I can only hope Irene did what I told her and locked her doors. Considering it may not be Larry Bennett. Home burglaries are a popular activity this time of year, with people's Christmas presents stacked neatly under the tree, all there for the taking.

If Larry Bennett killed Ebenita and they catch him in her house, Sammy could be free in a matter of hours. I should have asked Irene for a description. My heart skips an extra beat when I contemplate how we may be within moments of having the real killer in custody. With that mystery solved, all that's left is to locate a place to hold the Pedals of Promise event.

Minutes later, we pull up to Ebenita's house, where three police cars and Detective Rodriguez cruiser are parked - their lights flashing silently in the waning early evening light.

"What are the odds they agree to let us in?" Jack muses as we watch the hustle and bustle of law enforcement moving about the crime scene.

"I'm betting low," I grumble until I spot a friend.

"I know that guy." I point to one of the officers, a buddy from my days on the force. "Maybe he'll tell us something. Hey Tom," I call out as we approach. "What's happening?"

Tom looks uneasy, glancing over his shoulder before leaning closer. No doubt they've already warned him not to let us in. "Someone turned the place upside down. They were looking for something, Howie."

"So you didn't catch whoever it was?" I ask, the disappointment evident as I glance over to Mr. Bennett's house sitting dark and empty looking. I'm sorely tempted to knock on his door right now, but I fear that would only ensure unwanted police attention which I'm still avoiding at this point.

"Nope. They were gone by the time we got here."

"He didn't take anything?"

"Not from what we can tell so far. Whoever it was just tossed the place."

"Did Mrs. Jensen give you a description?"

He shakes his head sadly, thankfully ignoring the fact I've been talking with Irene. "Not really. She said it was too dark to tell."

"We need to see Detective Rodriguez."

"No can do, old friend. I'm under strict orders; no one goes in. No one bothers the detective. 'Not even her mother,' she told me."

Jack and I exchange a troubled look. She obviously knew in advance we'd want to poke around. But no one knows about the key I found at the crime scene – no one except possibly the burglar. What if that's what they were looking for? Guilt gnaws at me. I should've told Detective Rodriguez about it. The break-in changes everything.

"We need to get inside, Tom. It's important," I press, but he's firm. I should add I have something she needs to see but I don't.

"Sorry, Howie. Orders are orders." I give him a look, hoping to intimidate him as an elder, but he doesn't budge. "Between you and me. I'm a little afraid of Detective Rodriguez," he whispers.

You and me both, pal. And now I have to tell her I've secretly been carrying a potential piece of evidence in my pocket this whole time.

Chapter 20

Once we realize that hanging around the crime scene will only get us into more trouble than it's worth, Jack and I head back to Pizzazzle's. (I told you we wouldn't forget pizza forever.) The aroma of baking dough and simmering tomato sauce fills the air, a welcome distraction from our chaotic day. We order a large pepperoni pizza, the warmth of the box comforting in my hands on the way home.

When we finally get back to my house (after approximately three years, according to my dog), we happily witness Scooby's usual song and dance. His tail wags furiously, a blur of excited motion encompassing his entire body, while his eyes light with unmistakable joy, and he bounds straight for us with enthusiastic barks.

He's so excited to have company he can't decide who to greet first. I gasp when he leaps onto Jack's lap, covering his chin with kisses. "Scooby!" I scold.

"Oh, he's fine. I don't mind," Jack insists. "You know, the VA has approved me for a service dog."

"What? I didn't know you applied!" I tell him.

"It was a long time ago, and I didn't want to say anything until I got approved."

"Congratulations. That's exciting, man," I tell him, grasping his shoulder. "I would say get a dachshund, but it wouldn't be the most efficient dog for helping with tasks around the house. Their reach is rather limited." I laugh as Scooby, who has already returned to one of his beds for a quick nap, lifts his head, giving me the annoyed side-eye.

"Yeah, ideally, it should be a little higher than my ankles."

After I set out plates and napkins and grab two beers from the refrigerator, Jack and I belly up to the kitchen table. I barely open the box when Jack grabs a slice, his appetite undiminished by the day's events. "So, what's your take on all this?" he asks between bites.

I take a slice, too, but my appetite isn't quite as hearty as his.

"We need to visit Sammy tomorrow to learn what he has to say about the assault charges and the restraining order."

"I still say there's no way he assaulted Ebenita. Not a chance," Jack says, wiping his mouth with a napkin.

"And I agree, but if that's what Rodriguez insists is his motive we need to straighten it out. You're the lawyer, is there a mistake in the records somehow?"

"I wouldn't exactly say mistake, but sometimes they'll throw on as many charges as they can to see what sticks. It may have been something like that."

"But that would mean there was still some kind of issue with Ebenita where Sammy got arrested and she got a restraining order against him, but he didn't tell me. It doesn't make sense."

"Hey, I agree, and that's why I think it's a good idea to talk to him in person. Should we set a time now?"

Guilt gnaws at me. I haven't told Jack about the key and I don't know what Detective Rodriguez will do once I reveal it to her tomorrow. I may be sharing a cell with Sammy so Jack could visit us together.

"I have a few errands to run tomorrow first so why don't we play it by ear?"

"Works for me!" he exclaims. "And what are we going to do about the bikes we need to get out of the warehouse?" Jack continues.

"I still don't know and time is running short. I guess we could invite the families to drive up to the warehouse to pick up a bike."

"But then they don't get the meal or Santa or anything. It's just a bike," Jack points out.

"I hear you, but at this point we still haven't found a solution and I don't want those bikes to get destroyed when the demolition team shows up on the 26th."

"What about the families who can't drive to the warehouse to pick up the bike?" Jack asks.

"I could deliver them myself using my pickup."

"So there's that at least. The bikes won't be destroyed."

"Yeah. What a drag though. Who knew Ebenita's final act would be to torture as many of us as possible," I tell him.

Once Jack leaves and I ensure the house is locked tight, I return to the kitchen to wrap up the leftover pizza, which will make a tasty lunch tomorrow. Next, I load the dishwasher, wipe down the table, clear the kitchen counters, and consider vacuuming when I realize I'm only procrastinating. *You've put this off long enough*, I scold myself. It's time to call Detective Rodriguez and fess up. Besides, I do have important news about Larry Bennett.

I pick up the phone, my heart pounding, mentally reviewing the request I prepared - I'll suggest we meet in person tomorrow so I can hand over the key, but after all my mental gymnastics, it goes to voicemail anyway. I leave a brief message, my voice steady but tense. "Detective

Rodriguez, it's Howie O'Sullivan. I have some important news about the case. Are you free to meet tomorrow? Let me know. Thanks!"

No sooner do I hang up than my phone rings. Yikes. That was fast. Here goes nothing. Oh! Wait. It's Alastair McClellan. What remarkable timing.

"This is Howard O'Sullivan," I answer. Because I never met the guy I don't know if he's one of those *hey there Alastair* types.

"Ah, Mr. O'Sullivan, this is Alastair McClellan. You left me a message to call you."

"Yes, thanks for getting back to me. I found a key and was told you might be able to identify it."

"Ah, keys! They're like tiny metal whispers, holding secrets of doors unopened, chests unexplored. Do tell, is this key whispering to you, Mr. O'Sullivan?"

Whoa that's kind of freaky. How did he know? "Well, I'm not sure about whispering. It's just a key I found. I thought it might be important." No way I'm admitting to him it's practically haunting me.

"How thrilling! The drama of life and keys intertwining. You must bring this artifact to me. I dwell where the earth touches the sky, in the mountains, away from the prying eyes of civilization."

"Okay... Do you have time to meet tomorrow?"

"Tomorrow, when the sun kisses the peak of Mount Antero, come to my abode. It's where the dirt road dances with the wind. But beware, for my shop is not like others. It's a sanctuary where metal meets magic."

"Right, I'll be there. Thank you, Mr. McClellan. And what time would that be exactly?"

"9 a.m. Mr. O'Sullivan, one more thing. Bring an open mind and the key's secrets shall reveal themselves. Until then, let the anticipation simmer in your soul."

"I'll... keep that in mind. See you tomorrow."

"Farewell, seeker of truths locked away. Farewell!"

That night, my sleep is restless, filled with strange dreams where keys and locks morph into sinister symbols, and shadowy figures lurk just out of sight. I wake up unsettled, the images from my dreams lingering like a bad aftertaste.

Scooby and I go through our usual morning routine—potty break outside for him, coffee, and Frosted Mini Wheats for me. I contemplate the leftover pizza for breakfast but decide it will make a better lunch. Detective Rodriguez hasn't returned my call yet, but no doubt it's coming.

Once again, I apologize to Scooby for leaving him at home. McClellan's place is in the Gunbarrel area, nowhere near Mount Antero, so I'm not sure what that was about, but given what the locksmith said about him previously, plus our awkward conversation last night, I don't want to put Scooby into a problematic situation.

The drive to Gunbarrel takes me away from the familiar bustle of Boulder, leading me into a more secluded, almost hidden part of the area. Legend has it that it was once a stop on a stagecoach route, and that's where it got its name.

When I leave the paved roads behind, the landscape gradually shifts, the houses and shopping centers give way to more rustic and untamed scenery. The road narrows, eventually splitting into a winding dirt lane snaking its way through a dense thicket of trees, their branches forming a canopy overhead filtering the morning light into a dappled pattern on the ground.

The path is uneven, full of ruts and stones, making the drive a careful, slow progress. The sound of gravel crunching under my tires is a steady companion, punctuated by the occasional creak of the truck's suspension as it navigates the rougher patches.

As I round a final bend, McClellan's shop comes into view, an unassuming structure blending into its surroundings like a natural extension of the landscape. The shop's secluded location, tucked away in this quiet, almost hidden extension of Boulder, only makes it more mysterious, the perfect place for a craftsman of secrets and locks.

McClellan is as peculiar as I pictured him. His hair is unkempt, his eyes are sharp but distant, and his movements are erratic, like a character from an old mystery novel.

"Hello, Alastair? I'm Howie."

"Ah, the seeker arrives! Welcome to my realm of lost treasures and whispered secrets. The air here is thick with tales untold, isn't it?"

"Um, sure. It's... an interesting place. I brought the key you wanted to see."

"The key! The harbinger of mysteries locked away. Present it, let its metal sing its story to me."

"Here you go." After handing him the key he momentarily presses it to his chest before looking at it.

"Ah, exquisite! Each groove, each cut, a word in the diary of its existence. We shall unravel its narrative, Mr. O'Sullivan, fear not."

He examines the key closely, then looks up at me with a knowing gaze. "I made this key," he says in a gravelly voice. "It was for a custom cabinet commissioned by Loretta Kinsley."

"Wait. The antique dealer at Whispering Pines Antiquities?"

"Indeed, that's the one."

Chapter 21

I leave McClellan's place with more questions than answers. Last night, I was convinced the clues pointed to Larry Bennett as the killer. But what if it's Loretta Kinsley? This thing gets twistier by the moment.

Detective Rodriguez hasn't returned my call, so I rationalize that as an excuse to visit Whispering Pines Antiquities *before* turning the key over to the authorities. I'll tell Detective Rodriguez that I was simply looking into another credible suspect before meeting with her in person. I'm actually helping her. Yes, I'm sure she'll buy that. Better yet, maybe when I show Loretta the key she'll cave on the spot, admit to everything and turn herself in. I know. That never happens. But how great would it be if it did?

As I guide my truck back onto the main road, I'm grateful it didn't snow last night, allowing the plows to catch up—too many stubborn drivers out there refusing to respect an icy, snow-packed street. And that's putting it kindly. I've witnessed the aftermath of many horrific accidents where drivers fail to acknowledge the fact they're operating thousands of pounds of machinery, ignoring the slick and dangerous conditions. It isn't pretty.

The main road back to Boulder has two lanes on each side with a wide, grassy median between. Grassy in the summer, anyway. Right now, it's nothing but snow and mud. Traffic is surprisingly light for this time of day, allowing me to merge smoothly, the truck engine humming steadily beneath me. I'm surprised to discover I'm feeling pretty good right now despite the ever-deepening mystery. I still sense we've made a bit of progress. I just need to persuade Detective Rodriguez that we have two serious suspects beyond Sammy.

I adjust my rearview mirror, and that's when I notice it – a large silver pickup truck barreling down the lane behind me, closing the distance at an alarming rate. Its aggressive approach sets off alarms in my head, and I grip the steering wheel tighter, an uneasy feeling settling in my stomach. I try to maintain my speed and my lane, hoping the driver will pass by.

"Just use the left lane to pass me, you jerk," I mutter. But the truck doesn't pass. Instead, it veers dangerously close, its massive grill filling my mirror. "What the--" I sputter when the relentless driver hits my bumper. Struggling to keep my truck in the lane, I grip the steering wheel as tight as possible, but it's useless.

In the blink of an eye, my truck darts across the two lanes, tires skidding on the snow and ice piled along the edge of the median. I fight to regain control, but to no avail – I veer into the median as my world tilts violently. When the truck starts to flip, I brace myself, each roll a disorienting blur of gray skies, snow, and mud. While metal groans and glass shatters, my last thought is how profoundly grateful I am that Scooby isn't with me and I pray I didn't hit anyone else when I shot across the road.

When the chaos finally stops, and I land in the middle of the snowy median, the world is eerily silent except for the ticking of the engine, which has stopped running. Dazed and disoriented, my heart pounding against my ribs, I try to process what just happened.

Apparently, I'm not dead. Everything hurts, so that might actually be a good thing. I wiggle my fingers and toes for good measure, and they're still there. I thank my old, sturdy, tank-like truck for keeping me alive. Take that, all you naysayers who insisted I needed a new one.

Within seconds - or was it minutes, I'm so shaken and disoriented I can't tell - people call out, "Sir! Sir! Are you okay? He's moving! He's alive!" Their voices are a distant echo in my ears. I unbuckle my seat belt in an attempt to get out when I realize I'm stuck. How many times did I flip? I'm not pinned. I just can't get the door open.

"Sir! I'm a nurse! Don't move. Help is on the way!" a woman peering in through the broken window tells me.

"Is he bleeding?" someone asks.

"A little, but it doesn't look too bad."

Sirens that started in the distance quickly grow closer and then stop. Firefighters and paramedics sprint toward my car. I'm more alert now, and from what I can tell, I didn't break any bones. If only I could get the door open. Oh, no, they're prying it open with the jaws of life. Don't do that! This will be really expensive to repair.

"Sir! Hold still! We're getting you out!" a firefighter insists when I renew my struggle to get out on my own. After placing a C collar around my neck and despite my protests that I'm fine, they place me on a stretcher and load me into an ambulance. But not before I overhear a bystander insisting to one of the police officers the truck that ran me off the road did it purposely. I continue telling everyone around me I'm okay, but they ignore me. As we race down the road to Boulder Community Hospital, I think about how someone else will have to drive my truck home.

Once we arrive at the hospital, they poke and prod and subject me to an annoying number of tests for what seems like hours. After placing me in a curtained area and putting four stitches in my forehead, they come to the same conclusion I've been telling them all along. I'm fine. But when they demand I call someone to pick me up, I refuse, until I hear her. "Detective O'Sullivan! Please follow the doctor's orders."

"Detective Rodriguez!" I exclaim. "How did you know I was here?"

"My officers told me."

"I'm fine. I swear. See," I point to my forehead, "four stitches. That's all. It won't even leave a scar. But now that you're here, could you take me to my truck?"

Her pained expression tells me I don't want to hear what she says next. "The tow truck already took your vehicle."

"Oh good, do you know which body shop?" I stare at her expectantly. "What? Why are you looking at me like that?"

"You're *sure* he doesn't have a concussion?" she asks the doctor.

"I'm sure. CT scan was clear."

"Howie, your truck flipped three times."

"Three times? How is that possible?"

"I have a picture of it on the flatbed. I can show you if you want, but brace yourself," she says.

"Show me. I won't believe it until I see it." But when she starts to show me her phone, I put my hand up. "Wait. Maybe I don't want to see it."

"It's up to you, Detective."

"Okay, I'm ready. Let me see it."

When she holds her phone out to me, I shudder. How did I survive that? And I'm a little choked up, which I refuse to let her see when I realize my beloved truck is a goner.

"The officers told me two witnesses swear it looked like the truck that ran you off the road did so deliberately."

"Nah, I don't think so. The guy was just your run-of-the-mill aggressive driver. License plate?" I ask.

She shakes her head. "No license plate."

"Of course," I moan.

"So I got your message," she starts.

"Yes." I take a deep breath, stealing myself for the scolding (and possibly arrest!) that's about to come because I withheld evidence from the authorities. Then, I launch into my explanation of the key and what I learned about Larry Bennett and Loretta Kinsley. Detective Rodriguez is unhappy, to say the least, yet she's not quite as mad as I anticipated. I thought she might take me directly from the hospital to county lockup.

"And where is this key now?" she asks.

"It's in my pocket," I tell her, reaching for my pocket when I remember I'm wearing a hospital gown and not my clothes. "Uhhh," I mumble, scanning the area for them.

"Could you please hand me those?" I ask when I spot my clothes neatly folded on a chair in the corner.

"Sure thing," she says, handing them to me almost reluctantly like she's worried I'll change in front of her. There's zero chance of that, considering I'm embarrassed enough about wearing nothing but a hospital gown.

I dig in the right pocket of my pants, where I've been keeping the key since I found it and where I *know* I placed it after showing it to Alastair. It's not there! Maybe it's in the left pocket. Someone must have moved it when I got to the hospital. But it isn't there either.

"It's not here!" I exclaim, verging on panicking. Where *is* that key? "Excuse me! Nurse!" I bellow so obnoxiously that two nurses come running.

"There was a key in my pocket! Where is it?"

"Your car keys?" one of them asks.

"No!" I snap, then cringe because I sound so rude. "There was a large, handcrafted key in my pocket. It looks nothing like a car key."

"I'm sorry, sir, but there was no key in your pockets when they brought you in. Just your wallet and some lip balm," she explains, holding up a plastic bag with my wallet and my favorite cherry-flavored lip balm.

"Is there anyone else who could have my key?" I demand. I promise I'm not a jerk, but that key is essential.

"Howie," Detective Rodriguez says gently, laying a calming hand on my arm. "Maybe you should rest for a bit."

"I swear to you, I'm not making this up. I called you last night, long before the accident, and told you we needed to talk. I'm admitting to withholding evidence. You should be extra mad at me. Heck, maybe you should arrest me."

"I assure you, Howie, I'm furious at the thought of you withholding evidence, but I want to make sure you're okay before I yell at you too much—"

"But I—"

Detective Rodriguez holds her finger up when her ringing phone interrupts us. "Hang on, I have to take this. I promise, we'll discuss this later," she tells me before stepping away from the area to take the call.

"Sir, we're ready to discharge you," a nurse explains carefully as if he's anticipating another outburst from me, "but we can't let you leave on your own. Is there someone we can call for you?"

I peer through the curtain at Detective Rodriguez talking several yards away. Do I dare ask her to take me home? I don't want to bother her. Then it dawns on me if Ellie learns about the accident from someone else, I'll be in more trouble from her than I ever could be from Rodriguez.

"You can call my granddaughter," I tell him reluctantly.

"Why don't I do that while you get dressed?" he says, drawing the curtains closed, cutting off my view of Detective Rodriguez.

I quickly dress myself, turning out my pockets again, certain I must have missed the key somehow. I'm practically searching the floor on my hands and knees when Ellie flies in through the curtains.

"Gramps!" she cries, nearly knocking me over with her hug. I admit the adrenaline is wearing off, and I'm sore and tired. Perhaps a nap at home before I renew my search for the key?

On our way out, I apologize profusely to the nurses for getting so cranky and thank them for taking good care of me.

Ellie scolds me the entire way to her car about not calling her sooner, but I barely hear her. I can't stop thinking about that blasted key. It must have fallen out of my pocket during the accident. Is it in my mangled truck? Is it lying somewhere in the median? And where is Detective Rodriguez? She must have snuck out without telling me.

"Gramps!" Ellie waves her hand in front of my face. "Can you hear me? Are you sure you're okay?"

"I'm fine, Ellie, just a bit shaken up. But I'll warn you now, I'm without a truck for the time being, and I might need your help getting around for a bit," I admit, trying to downplay the seriousness of the accident.

"You're not going anywhere," she scolds. "Except right home to bed."

"I hardly think the bed is necessary," I try to tell her as she opens the passenger door for me. "How about this. I'll crash on the couch and watch TV the rest of the day."

"All right," she reluctantly agrees.

When we arrive home, Scooby is thrilled to see us as always. "You could give Scooby his lunch," I tell her while I take off my shoes and lie on the couch. "And could you hand me the remote?" I could learn to like this.

After feeding Scooby, she sits in the chair across from me. "What about *your* lunch?" she asks.

"I'd take a sandwich from Snarfs."

"You aren't just trying to get rid of me?"

"I swear I'm not." (I'm really not. That bowl of Mini Wheats was a long time ago.)

"Fine. Two sandwiches coming right up. But I swear if I get back and you aren't here..."

"I will be in this same spot when you return," I insist, changing the channel on the TV to prove how invested I am in resting for the remainder of the day.

"Okay, I'll be right back," she tells me.

My body aches from the crash, and a quick nap while Ellie is out would be heavenly. But just as I start to drift off, there's a knock at the door. Did she forget her key again? How long was I out? I shuffle to the door, opening it without a second thought.

But it isn't Ellie.

Standing on my porch is none other than Ebenita's neighbor Larry Bennett.

Chapter 22

Bennett looms in the doorway, larger and more imposing than I remember when I was the one standing on *his* porch. I swear he fills up the entire door frame, and his unkempt beard only makes him more intimidating, almost bear-like. He's a mountain of a man, and with the lingering aches from the car accident, I doubt I could hold my own against him.

For a fleeting moment, my mind jumps to the gun I keep in my nightstand and the baseball bat hidden just behind the door. (What? I'm an ex-cop!) Could I reach either in time if things turn south? Scooby went with Ellie to get sandwiches; otherwise, I could count on him to bark up a storm, then hide under the couch.

Larry's small black eyes fix on me, unblinking, the air between us crackling with tension. I can almost hear my heart hammering in my chest while the bruises from the crash throb with renewed intensity. I swallow hard, trying to appear calm and collected, but inside, I'm weighing my options for self preservation, praying the situation doesn't escalate. In this moment, standing on my doorstep with Larry Bennett, I feel the vulnerability of my age and my recent brush with death all too acutely.

Just as I'm about to ask him what he's doing on my porch using what I hope is an intimidating voice, he points to my head. "Dude. What happened to you?"

I self-consciously reach for the butterfly bandage covering the stitches on my forehead. That's when I recall hearing someone at the accident claim the truck ran me off the road on purpose. I also remember telling Detective Rodriguez how ridiculous that was, and yet here I am, staring up at the man who may have killed Ebenita, and he knows where I live.

"Do you drive a truck?" I ask.

"Huh?"

"A truck! A pickup! Do you have one?" I bark at him, standing as tall as I can, which still isn't a match for Larry.

"Yeah," he responds, his forehead furrowed in confusion. "It's right there." He turns and points to a small, older model, red pickup parked in front of my house while I breathe a sigh of relief (for the moment, anyway). "What happened to you?" he points at my forehead again.

"I was in a car accident."

"Oh, that's bad."

"What are you doing at my house?" I ask him.

"Huh? Oh, yeah, I was leaving you a note. I wasn't sure if you were home."

"Why?" I can't believe we're even having this conversation. Is he here to kill me or not?

"So, I've been wanting to tell you that I lied to you the other day about being at work and I've been feeling bad about it ever since."

Huh. This is a first. I've never had a suspect show up at my house to confess to lying about an alibi.

"So where were you when Ebenita was murdered?"

"I was in Blackhawk gambling at the casino. I have proof," he says, holding out a tax receipt from the Rocky Mountain Royale Casino.

I cautiously lean forward to read the receipt, still leery this is a trick of some sort. But there it is in black and white, his name, the date, and even the time stamp, which reads 12:01 AM. At 12:01, while someone killed Ebenita, Larry was winning $7500 at the roulette table in Blackhawk, Colorado.

"So why didn't you just tell me that when I first asked?"

"Because I was embarrassed that I got fired. And I had no idea who you were, so I panicked and told you the first thing that popped into my head. It was scary to think my next-door neighbor was murdered. Even though I admit I won't miss her for a second, you get my drift? But how did I know that *you* weren't the murderer?"

"What about the $15,000 you stole from work?"

"I gave it back. Technically, I barely even stole it. It was really stupid, but I was desperate. Ebenita dragged me in and out of court for years, man. And then she finally won her lawsuit. For $15,000! That's a lot of money! I didn't know what to do. Where would I get that kind of dough? And then it hit me. Do you know what kind of cash they keep at the pot store? It's wild. The truth is, I didn't think my plan would actually work, but when it did, I was shocked. There I was, walking out the door with $15,000, and it freaked me out. So you know what I did? I turned around and took it right back. But then I got caught."

"And you were arrested," I point out.

"More like 'shown the door' - they decided not to press charges since I brought it right back. Like, I literally didn't even make it to my car."

I'd argue that the fact he gave the money back could make it look even more likely that he killed her, but the receipt is legit. And as relieved as I am to learn I probably don't have a killer on my doorstep, it means I have one less credible suspect.

"So, anyway, I just wanted you to know that. I'm not a murderer. And I'm not a thief. Well, I am, but I'm not. I guess I'm not a very good thief."

"Okay, so, good to know. I appreciate your telling me." What am I supposed to say to the man? *Great! Have a nice day!* What a weird conversation this is turning out to be.

"Okay." He throws his hands in the air. "That's all I came to say. But you should probably rest so you can recover from your accident."

"Yes, I'll do that," I tell him. At 67 years old, that was one of the strangest conversations I've ever had. And that's saying something, given my recent conversation with Alastair.

I'm still standing on the porch, dumbfounded over what just happened, while I try to figure out what it means for this case, when Ellie returns with our lunch. I try ducking back inside before she sees me, but I'm too slow.

"Ah ha! You're planning to go somewhere. I knew it." She accuses.

"I swear I was trying to nap until you got home, but then Larry Bennett showed up."

"Ebenita's neighbor was at the house? Did you call the police? Did he threaten you? What happened? Are you all right?"

"You won't believe this, but he came here to admit he lied about his alibi."

"And *you* believe him?" she shrieks so loudly Scooby barks in protest.

I told her she wouldn't believe me. "He had a receipt from the Blackhawk casino where he was gambling at midnight when Ebenita was killed."

"And he came here, in person, to tell you this?"

"Yes! It was the weirdest thing. He also admitted to stealing the money from the pot store, but he took it back right away so they didn't press charges."

"I can't leave you alone for five minutes, can I?" she groans.

As soon as Ellie and I finish eating lunch, she insists I go upstairs for a nap, which I secretly admit sounds really good right now, but before I can do anything else, there's another knock at the door.

"This time, I get it!" Ellie insists.

"Not without finding out who it is first!" I scold. It's bad enough *I* keep opening the door without checking who's on the other side first. She *really* shouldn't.

"It's Jack!" she exclaims after peering through the peep-hole. "Did you tell him about the accident?"

"Nope."

"Someone obviously did."

As Ellie opens the door, Jack launches himself into my living room, concern etched across his face. "I heard about the accident. Are you all right? Why didn't you call me? Why did I have to see it on the news?"

"It was on the news?" I ask.

"Yes! With pictures of your destroyed truck... Sorry about that," he says when I cringe. "I freaked when I saw it. I can't believe you're standing here in front of me like it's any other day."

Ellie, hovering nearby, interjects, "Gramps is supposed to be resting, Jack."

"I'm okay, Ellie." I wave her concern away. "There's a lot we have to catch up on."

She frowns at me but relents. Wow, she looks like her mother when she does that!

"Make it quick. I'm watching the clock," she growls.

"Duly noted," I tell her before turning back to Jack. "I've been keeping a secret."

"From?" he asks.

"From everybody. Except Ellie. She was with me when I found it. And now Detective Rodriguez knows."

"Knows what? Found what? Why are you talking in code?"

"I found a custom-made key at the crime scene."

"Really?" Jack looks confused. "Greg hasn't mentioned a key."

"That's because I took it."

His mouth falls open. "You removed evidence from a crime scene? And before the cops arrived? Are you mad? What if you compromised Sammy's case?"

I hold my hand up. "For the record, I didn't find it *before* the authorities arrived. I found it hours after they left."

"Isn't that splitting hairs?"

"Maybe. But for all we know, it wasn't even a part of the crime scene. Who knows how long it was there? It may have nothing to do with the crime." Yes, I'm grabbing at excuses.

"Then why keep it a secret?" Jack squints at me.

"My point is, I found a custom-made key, and I took it." I show him the picture on my phone.

"Detective Rodriguez knows about this, and she hasn't killed you yet? Or at least arrested you?"

"It may have helped that I told her when I was lying on a hospital bed."

"So she has the key now?"

"Not exactly." I wiggle my hand.

"Define exactly."

"It's missing. Maybe lost."

"Am I being punked?" Jack asks Ellie, who shakes her head sadly.

"All right, so what else are you keeping from me?"

"A locksmith in town told me about an artisan steel-worker in Gunbarrel named Alastair. He insisted this Alastair person would know all about the key, so I drove up there this morning, and not only did he recognize the key, but he said he made it for Loretta Kinsley."

"The antique dealer Greg had you check into, who fought with Ebenita on the Pearl Street Mall, then sent her threatening emails, *and* had suspicious looking boots in her store?"

"The same."

"That makes her a suspect!"

"I know!"

"You have to tell Detective Rodriguez!"

"I did."

"And?" Jack stares at me, exasperated. "Has anyone ever told you that you're really annoying as an interviewee?"

"Actually, Detective Rodriguez told me that."

"Let's just get down to the nitty-gritty. What does she think of this, and how has she not arrested you already?"

"I don't know." I shrug. "The last time I saw her was in the hospital. She was definitely annoyed, but then she got a call and left. I haven't heard from her since."

"Please tell me that's it," Jack says, looking from me to Ellie and back again.

"What?" he sighs after seeing our expressions.

I recount my story of Larry Bennett's visit, playing down the part about Bennett's size. Jack doesn't need to know I nearly wet my pants when I saw Larry standing on my porch.

"I can't believe you did all this in one day." He moans, removing his baseball cap and running his hands through his hair. "And we still need to talk to Sammy!"

"Yes!" I exclaim. "What time is it? Are visiting hours still open?"

"Absolutely not!" Ellie declares while Scooby runs around her feet, barking in agreement. "Jack, it's time for you to go home. Gramps, you need to rest. You were in a severe accident today, yet you're acting like it's your average afternoon."

"Ellie, honey, I appreciate your concern, but it's crucial we solve this. Time is running out." Given the look on her face, I realize right away I shouldn't have said it like she's still six years old.

"Howie, Ellie is right. You're still working on adrenaline, and it won't help anyone if you collapse and end up back in the hospital. Rest tonight, and we'll hit it again with a fresh start tomorrow, okay? We'll meet with Sammy and get to the bottom of *that* story anyway."

Scooby barks again. Outvoted 3 to 1. Man's best friend indeed. I scowl at him.

After seeing Jack out to his car, Ellie returns with a duffle bag. "What's in that?"

"Just some things I need to stay the night. I picked them up when I got our lunch."

"Oh, great, now I need a babysitter."

"If you want to call it that," she says.

"Fine," I grumble flopping back onto the couch and turning on Wheel of Fortune. But if she thinks she's keeping me home tomorrow, she's got another thing coming.

Chapter 23

I wake up with the morning light filtering through the curtains, my body aching in protest at the stark reminder of yesterday's harrowing ordeal. I sit up slowly, expecting the usual slurpy greeting from Scooby, but the room is empty. Where is he? He always wakes *me* up. I don't like this one bit. What happened to my dog?

Pulling myself out of bed, I shuffle downstairs, as fast as I can manage, but each step is a test of endurance. When I reach the kitchen, the aroma of breakfast fills the air. I forgot Ellie stayed over! She's bustling around the kitchen, skillfully flipping pancakes and setting the table. Scooby sits obediently at her feet, his eyes following her every move, his paws crossed in anticipation that she'll accidentally, on purpose, drop a bite or two for him.

"Morning, Ellie," I call out with relief, but surprised when my voice comes out a little hoarse.

"Morning, Gramps. Sit down," she chirps, glancing over her shoulder, her beautiful smile lighting up her face. "Breakfast's almost ready."

The table is a spread of hearty fare – fluffy pancakes, scrambled eggs, golden toast, fresh fruit, and a pot of coffee. I slide into a chair, my stomach rumbling in anticipation.

"Hey, where's the bacon?" I complain.

"I'm sure you get plenty of bacon otherwise. I think you can skip it for a day."

I don't want to sound like a grumpy old man. It's not every day I wake up to a mouth-watering breakfast like this right in my own kitchen. Actually, I *never* wake up to a breakfast like this in my kitchen unless I'm the one making it. But I miss my bacon!

"Why don't you stay home and take it easy for another day?" Ellie suggests. "I could call out sick from the bookstore, and we can hang together, pop some popcorn, and watch old movies?"

I reach across the table to pat her hand. "I swear that sounds wonderful, and I would love to do that with you soon, but Jack and I have to go to the prison today to see Sammy and then to Kinsley's antique shop."

"I figured that's how you'd answer, but please be careful today and try to take it easy, alright? What would Scooby and I do without you?"

"I don't think you'll have to worry about that for quite some time," I assure her. "I'm like a cat."

"Just don't use up too many lives in one week, okay?"

"Deal!" I tell her as the doorbell rings, and Scooby runs to the door, barking like a maniac. "That must be Jack."

"I'll get it," she says, thankfully, peering through the peephole first. "Yep!"

"Gramps tells me you're getting a service dog," she says after Jack rolls into the house. "How exciting!"

He beams with anticipation. "I'm really looking forward to it. And yet, I'm nervous at the same time. It's a lot of help but a lot of responsibility, too."

"I'm sure you two will be great for each other," she assures him.

"Come get some breakfast, Jack!" I call out.

"Bacon?" he says while Ellie shakes her head at us.

"No bacon, but plenty of everything else," I tell him.

"Set me up, please!" he says, rolling over to the table.

For a while, the only sounds we hear are the three of us inhaling Ellie's delicious breakfast. "Okay, I have a question no one has answered yet," she says, breaking the silence. "Did Sammy try to order a ride share? The cab companies say there's no record of him contacting them, yet we're sure he didn't walk home. He rented an e-bike, after all; why not order a ride share?"

"That's an excellent idea and one of the first things we thought of," Jack says, "but he left his phone at home in his drunken stupor. He had his wallet, which he used to rent the bike, but he couldn't order a ride share without his phone."

"Oh, shoot, I thought I might be on to something," she laments.

"Hang on a second," I interrupt. "Maybe you *are* on to something."

"What do you mean?" Jack asks, shoveling another forkful of eggs into his mouth.

"Just because the cab company doesn't have a *record* of picking up Sammy doesn't mean a cabbie never did."

"He flagged down a cabbie who picked him up off book, maybe?" Ellie suggests.

"Ellie, you're brilliant!" I tell her.

"Now we just have to figure out which one," Jack reminds us.

"I'll leave that up to you two," Ellie says, excusing herself from the table. "And since I cooked, you gentlemen have the honor of cleaning the kitchen— I have to go to work," she says, grabbing her car keys and coat. "Call me if you need anything." She shakes her finger at me. "And we need to look for a new truck for you."

I nod, understanding the necessity but dreading the process. "Thanks, Ellie. We'll sort it out."

"Visiting hours start at 10," Jack says after she closes the door behind her.

"Let's get a move on then," I tell him. "Oh. After we clean up!"

We push through the heavy doors into the prison visiting area, my footsteps echoing off the dingy walls while Jack wheels along silently. The space is stark, the air heavy with a sense of desolation. The fluorescent lights above cast a harsh glow, stripping away any warmth. Jack's chair won't fit in Sammy's narrow cell, so we're meeting him in the visitor's area this time.

Moments later, when they escort the inmates into the visiting room, the sight of Sammy is alarming. He looks like a shell of the man I knew. His face is drawn, and his eyes are sunken, surrounded by dark circles. His usual neat appearance is long gone, replaced by a disheveled, unkempt look. Prison life has taken its toll on him in just a few days. I shiver when I contemplate him having to spend much longer in here. Would he even survive?

"Hey, guys. Hope you're here with good news," he says quietly, offering us a weak smile.

Jack nods sympathetically. "We're doing what we can, Sammy."

Sammy's gaze shifts to me, noticing the bruises from the accident. "Saw the news about your crash, Howie. Are you okay? I was worried."

"I'm good. But I'm afraid my old truck is done for."

"Oh, no!" Sammy moans. "You love that truck."

"Yeah, but at least it's something that can be replaced. Kind of anyway." I cringe when I say it, having failed to convince myself yet that a new truck is necessary.

"Please tell me Scooby wasn't with you."

"He wasn't, thank goodness. I was also blessed with light traffic, so no one else was injured."

"What happened?"

"Just some jerk aggressive driver ran me off the road."

"Ellie mentioned some of the witnesses were convinced it was deliberate," Jack adds.

"Deliberate!" Sammy exclaims.

"Who would want to run *me* off the road? It wasn't deliberate," I respond, shaking my head. "We'll get right to the point," I tell Sammy, pulling out a copy of the record

I found online. "Why didn't you tell me about the assault charge and the restraining order Ebenita filed against you?"

His expression falters. "Because it wasn't assault, you guys. A friend and I spray painted her house in a moment of anger. And that restraining order? It was never granted."

"So what happened, exactly? And why?" I press. How did they get an assault charge from spray paint? And why in heaven's name did they do that in the first place?

"Ebenita claims she slipped and fell at the Flourish & Batter Bakery." Sammy starts.

"Oh, I remember that place. They had really good bread. Didn't it go out of business? What happened?"

"Ebenita is what happened."

"Uh oh."

"But what does that have to do with you?" Jack asks.

"The owner, Stanley, was a good friend of mine."

"So what did Ebenita do?"

"She claimed she slipped on a banana peel."

"That's a joke, right?" Jack asks.

"We thought so too at first. Which only infuriated her. The next thing Stanley knew, Ebenita was suing him for $250,000. The insurance company insisted on settling but then raised his rates so much he couldn't afford to stay in the business."

"Ebenita seems to have made a business from suing people," I point out.

"Yep," Sammy says.

"Then what happened?"

"We were convinced it was a scam, so he hired a private investigator to follow her."

"Don't tell me..." Jack trails off.

"You got it. The private investigator confirmed she was faking the injury."

"Then the insurance company got their money back!" I exclaim.

"Nope." Sammy shakes his head. "They said it wasn't worth pursuing. Insisted it would cost more to pursue her for fraud than just letting it go."

"Meanwhile, your friend pays the price," I groan.

"Exactly. So we spray painted the word FRAUD in glow in the dark paint on her front door. I admit it was immature. We plead guilty to vandalism and did community service."

"Why do the public records show it as assault?" I ask, confused.

"Those were the initial charges that Ebenita wanted pinned on us, which everyone, including the judge, said were bogus. He changed the record to reflect the proper charge and immediately dismissed the request for a restraining order. Why it shows up like that in the public records is beyond me. That would be a question for Greg."

I'm relieved we finally have answers. Not that I believed he assaulted her, but we still had to confirm what happened, and I'm glad we waited to get the explanation straight from Sammy.

Recalling the conversation with Ellie this morning, I continue my line of questioning. "Do you remember how you got home that night?" I ask, searching his face for any clue of recognition.

He shakes his head, a look of genuine confusion crossing his features. "I don't, Howie. It's all a blur."

"And the bike you rented," I press on, knowing Greg would have discussed this with him already. "How did it end up behind the dumpster at the crime scene?"

Sammy's shoulders slump, his frustration evident. "I wish I knew. I remember nothing about that bike after I left Ebenita's."

I lean forward, my voice firm. "Sammy, you need to try to remember. That bike being found at the scene – it connects you to the murder."

He looks down, his hands clenched. "I'm trying, Howie. I really am. But I can't seem to get past the gap in my memory." I'm taken aback when Sammy's face turns brooding. "You know, when they said I had visitors, I got so excited. I was sure you had good news for me. Instead, you've spent our time grilling me. You even had to ask me if I assaulted someone. Something both of you should know I'd never do. Especially a woman. Even if it was Ebenita."

"We swear, we know you're innocent, and we never once thought you could have assaulted Ebenita," Jack insists.

"Then why are you here?" Sammy says, leaping up angrily. "We're done. Guard, take me back to my cell."

Chapter 24

W hen Jack and I approach Whispering Pines Antiquities we're stunned by the sign in the window. "Going Out of Business Sale."

"What on earth?" Jack mutters.

"If that isn't suspicious, I don't know what is," I tell him.

"You think she's looking to get out of dodge?" Jack asks.

"I sure do."

"You're closing your shop?" I blurt out the moment I spot Loretta behind the counter. She fought Ebenita tooth and nail to keep this place, yet now that Ebenita is gone and no longer a threat, she quits? Unless she's planning to run, it makes no sense.

"Yes," she sighs. "I was afraid you'd act this way. I was hoping I wouldn't have to see you before I left."

"I bet," Jack mumbles under his breath.

"Why are you closing the shop?" I ask.

"I'm just done, you know. Tired of the bureaucracy and the lawyers and the fights. I called the corporation that owns the remainder of the development and asked what they would pay for my place. We signed the paperwork yesterday, and I'm buying a ranch in Montana. I take it you aren't here to ask me about my retirement plans, though."

"You know how suspicious this looks, right?" I continue to press.

"Suspicious, as in I killed Ebenita?"

"Yes!"

"I already told you I didn't kill her."

I pull out my phone to show her a picture of the key. "Do you recognize this?"

She pales as her eyes flick to the screen, then dart away. "No," she says sharply.

"Are you sure?" I ask, staring her down while she continues to look away.

"Yes," she replies.

"Alastair told me he made it just for you."

The admission seems to shift something in her demeanor. "Alright, yes. He made it for a cabinet I refinished."

"Can we see the cabinet?" Jack asks.

"No."

"Why not?"

"It's not here anymore."

Why is she being so cagey about this? Something is really off about her.

"Where is it?" I swear if she tells me she doesn't know…

"I sold it."

"To?" Jack throws his hands in the air.

After a pause so lengthy that I'm ready to start tossing the place, looking for it, she responds so quietly I barely hear her, "I sold it to Ebenita."

"What? Ebe --" I'm cut short when my phone rings. Normally, I'd ignore it in a moment like this, but it's Greg, and my heart sinks. What if something has happened? Our visit with Sammy has weighed heavily on me since we left lockup, and now Kinsley is messing with us. I don't know how much more bad news I can stand.

"I have to take this," I tell Jack and Loretta before ducking outside.

"Hey, Greg." I sigh.

"We may have a break," he announces.

I stand up straighter, alert. "What's going on?"

"As you already know, after you messaged me with your theory about a cab driver picking up Sammy the night Ebenita was murdered, I had my intern call every cab company she could find, looking for a driver who may have picked up someone off-book the night Ebenita was murdered."

"And?" I answer, my heart racing.

"Not only were you right, I think we've found the guy," Greg explains, his voice tinged with cautious optimism.

A surge of hope courses through me. "That's great news. Where do I find him?"

"He'll meet you at Bean Mystique Cafe on Canyon Boulevard."

"I'm on my way!" I exclaim.

"Slow down a second. He's very reluctant to talk to anyone official because he doesn't want his boss to know. He only contacted us after overhearing the receptionist talking to my intern, so he wrote down the number and called. He's adamant that no one at his company finds out what he did."

"Why the secrecy?" I ask. "This sounds sketchy."

"He claims he's worried if his company finds out he picked up someone and didn't charge him, he could be fired."

"I hope that's all it is," I tell him.

"You and me both. That's why I want *you* to question this guy. We must make sure he's credible. If our case comes down to this witness, his testimony has to be solid. We have to know we can trust him."

"Do we have a name or phone number for him?"

"Nope. Just that he's waiting for you at the coffee shop. I need you to get over there before he gets nervous and bolts."

"Copy. I'll meet with him now," I respond, suddenly feeling the weight of the responsibility and hopeful all at once. "I'll get the truth out of him."

"Let me know what he says."

"Of course!"

"Hey, Jack. Can you drop me off at the Bean Mystique Cafe?" I ask after hanging up with Greg.

"Uh, yeah, when?"

"Now."

"Now? I thought we were uh..." he nods in Loretta's direction who's looking increasingly nervous. As much as I want to stay and question her, I can't be in two places at once, and the cab driver takes precedence. If this cab driver has to wait too long and runs before I can question him, I'll never forgive myself. I just hope Loretta doesn't take off either. This was so much easier when I had an entire police force to help me.

"We'll be back," I tell her while signaling to Jack we need to leave now. I want her uneasy and on edge. She's more likely to confess that way.

"We may have our first break," I whisper to Jack.

"What? I'll come with you."

"No. I need to tackle this one alone. Greg found a witness. A cab driver who's skittish and worried about losing his job. We don't know his name or where he lives. Just think, if his account holds up, it could be the piece of evidence that shifts the entire case. Sammy's freedom might hinge on what happens next."

"Let's go!' Jack declares.

I convince him to drop me off across the street from the coffee shop so I can approach alone and on foot. I'm not taking any chances with the man I've taken to calling Cabbie in my head since I don't know his real name.

When I push open the door to the Bean Mystique Café, I barely notice the aroma of fresh coffee surrounding me. Normally, I'd stop for an Americano, but it's all business today. I scan the room, looking for a nervous stranger, when I spot him tucked away in a corner booth, fidgeting with a cup. Our eyes meet, and his apprehension is palpable. That has to be Cabbie.

"Hi, I'm Howie O'Sullivan with Baxter, Sterling & Dunn. I'm here to talk to you about the passenger you picked up a few nights ago."

He nods, indicating I should sit down at his table. "You have to promise me this won't leave here," he says so quietly I can barely hear him. "The company has a zero-tolerance policy when it comes to off-book fares. If they found out I picked one up, and now there's a law firm sniffing around about it, they'd fire me for sure. I can't afford to lose my job."

I hold up my hand. "I'm only interested in building a timeline. The man in question. The man who I think you picked up is my best friend. So, I'm not just an investigator with the law firm. This is really important to me."

He nods with understanding before starting his tale. "As I'm sure you know, it was snowing and bitter cold that night, and boy, was it quiet. I really count on fares this time of year. People are in a good mood, they're at parties, they're eating and drinking, and it's cold, so they're happy to get in a toasty warm cab..."

I flashback to how nice the working heater felt in Detective Rodriguez's car compared to how cold it always is in my truck, and I could see why people tip well. I guess that will be one of the benefits of a new truck - a working heater.

"...but that night was painfully slow. I only had one fare, and it was a lousy tip too. I was circling the area near the Starlight Community Center, wondering why I was even bothering when I saw something... or rather, someone."

He pauses as if replaying the scene in his head. "There was this guy struggling with a bike in the snow. A bike!

For a second, I thought I was losing my mind. I had to be hallucinating, right? It's cold and snowing, and yet there's some dude with a bike. But something was wrong with it. He looked like he was trying to repair it or something."

I nod knowingly. The cold must have been too much for the bike's battery. I lean in to hear him better, my heart racing. This is it. This is our alibi. I bet the cabbie picked up Sammy right after Irene Jensen saw him at Ebenita's." What did you do?" I ask.

"I pulled up beside him, thinking maybe *he* was the one who was out of his mind," Cabbie continues. "But once I got out of the cab, I could smell the alcohol, and that's when I knew he was drunk. He was barely able to stand straight. I knew I couldn't just leave him there; he would've frozen to death. I even thought about calling an ambulance, but I wasn't sure how long that would take, and I was certain he didn't have much time left in the cold."

"So, you offered him a ride?" I prompt.

"Yeah. I figured he didn't have any money on him, but I couldn't in good conscience leave him out there."

"What did you do with the bike?"

Suddenly I'm nervous. I can already hear Detective Rodriguez. If they left the bike where he picked up Sammy, she would insist they still needed to know who put the bike behind the dumpster.

"I didn't want his bike to get stolen, but I didn't have room in the cab. I suggested we stash it behind the trash dumpster. I figured as cold as it was, no one would be out looking to steal it. I hoped that he would remember it the next day and retrieve it."

It's all I can do to keep from jumping up and down and cheering. Who cares that Cabbie obviously didn't realize it was a rental. *He* put the bike behind the dumpster.

"This will sound like a strange question, but did you see anyone else hanging around, looking suspicious?"

"Uh, no, why are you asking me that?"

"No reason. It's not important," I respond hastily. The last thing I need to do is scare this guy when he's ready to give me the necessary answers. "So you put the bike behind the dumpster, and then what? Sammy got in the cab? Where did you take him?"

"He insisted I take him to the Veteran's Hearth Bar. I told him I thought he'd had enough to drink as it was and why don't I take him home instead? But he insisted he owned the place!"

"Yeah, he actually does."

"Well, don't that beat all. Anyway, I drove him to the bar. When we got there, he pulled a $100 bill from his wallet, insisting I take it."

I raise an eyebrow. "Did you?"

He looks away momentarily, then back at me. "I tried to refuse, but he was adamant, kept saying I saved his life. It was Christmas, and he was so insistent. So, I took it and didn't report it, which is why no one else can know about this. I could plead my case with my boss if I swore I saved a guy from freezing. But if they learned about the $100, I didn't report..." He makes a slashing motion across his throat.

"I understand." I sit back, processing his story. "Did he say anything else during the ride? Anything that might help explain why he was there with the bike?"

The cab driver shakes his head. "Not much. He was too drunk to make a lot of sense. Just kept thanking me."

"And what time did you pick him up?"

"It would have been a little after 1 a.m."

"Oh." That's not what I expected. I've let this case get too personal. I didn't think to confirm the time *first* as I normally would have done. As his words sink in, I grapple with the heavy weight settling in my chest. The fragile thread of hope I'd been clinging to has disappeared in an instant.

"1:00? Are you absolutely certain? You're sure it wasn't more like 11:00?"

He laughs. "I'm certain. I get off work at 2:00, so that's how I knew. When I looked at the clock, I thought, well,

I have less than an hour left. If it was only 11:00, I would have remembered that."

So that's two people who can place Sammy near the crime scene an hour *after* Ebenita was murdered. That doesn't help much. But at least now we have an answer for how the bike got stashed behind the dumpsters.

If I'm going to solve this case once and for all, I need to determine why Mrs. Jensen said 11:00, and Mr. Kowalski said 1:00. One of them is wrong.

Chapter 25

That's it. It's time for me to finally sew up this bizarre event sequence. When exactly was Sammy at Ebenita's house, and more importantly, when wasn't he? I refuse to accept the notion he was there twice. Especially on a bike in the snow. Someone is either mistaken or lying, and I won't leave that neighborhood until I have the truth.

Seeing Sammy in prison today shocked me. I had hoped he would adjust at least somewhat after a few days, but it's the opposite. He's declining rapidly, and I have to get him out of there.

Thankfully, Ebenita's neighborhood is within walking distance from the coffee shop, so I don't have to call anyone for a ride. As much as I hate to admit it, I need a new truck. And soon. I haven't had to ask people for rides since I was a teenager, and I don't like it one bit.

When I ring Mrs. Jensen's doorbell, I can't help but smile when it plays Jingle Bells.

"Hello, Mrs. Jensen!"

"Why, hello, Mr. O'Sullivan. Please come in. Are you here for more cookies?"

"No. Well, actually, they were delicious." Normally, I wouldn't bother. I'd get right to business. But gosh, those cookies were good.

"Coming right up," she declares, scurrying into the kitchen.

Now I'm mortified. I didn't mean for her to run off and get cookies when I have far more pressing things on my mind.

"Truthfully, Mrs. Jensen, I came to double check—"

"Hello." A man, who I'm assuming is Mr. Jensen, greets me.

"Hello!" I tell him.

"Mr. O'Sullivan, this is my husband, Lester."

"Hello there, nice to meet you."

"Mr. O'Sullivan came to get more cookies."

"Okay." Lester looks at me strangely.

I laugh nervously. "Actually, my reason for this visit is to talk to you about the man you saw at Ebenita's. More specifically I'd like to discuss the time."

"11:00 pm." she insists again.

Rats.

"No, that's not right," Mr. Jensen says.

"Of course, it's right, dear."

"I told you this already. The power was out earlier that night, and you forgot to reset the clock by the bed."

"How long was the power out?" I ask.

"About two hours."

So that's it. Mrs. Jensen and Mr. Kowalski saw Sammy at Ebenita's house at 1 a.m.

"Here you go, dear." She smiles, handing me a package of cookies wrapped with a red ribbon.

"Thank you so much. You really didn't have to give me more cookies," I tell her.

"Nonsense. I'm delighted when my baking makes someone happy."

As I make my way to the front door, maneuvering around all the Christmas decorations (I'm convinced there are even more than last time) Mr. Pickles peeks at me from around the corner. When Mrs. Jensen turns her back for a moment, I stick my tongue out at him.

"By the way," I pause at the Jensen's front door, "let me know if you see any suspicious activity next door at Ebenita's."

"Absolutely!"

"Do not, under any circumstances, go over there or confront anyone you might see, but please call me right away, okay?"

"I will stay alert!" Mrs. Jensen assures me.

"I don't doubt it!" I tell her.

As I stroll down the Jensen's walkway, my mind awhirl with thoughts of everything that's happened today, a massive silver pickup truck with tinted windows obscuring the driver, slows down in front of the house, but the moment I lift my head, it quickly drives away.

It crosses my mind that it looked an awful lot like the truck that ran me off the road yesterday. *Could* it have been on purpose? But why? Sure, I made plenty of enemies while on the force, but who? And why now of all times? I trudge home, trying to sort out everything in my brain. Ever since we were at the antique shop, and I pulled up the photo of the key to question Ms. Kinsley with, I've had this inkling of a crucial piece of the puzzle lurking just out of reach in the corner of my mind, elusive and shadowy. It's like a frustrating whisper, indistinct, refusing to crystallize. It's teasing me, promising answers, if only I could figure out what it is.

I often find that reviewing crime scene photos jogs my memory, forcing me to focus.

Once I get home and apologize profusely to Scooby for neglecting him the last couple of days, I dig out the photos I printed at Walgreens. I'm mesmerized by pictures of the footprints in the snow when something hits me. It's still there, just out of reach, yet a bit clearer now. I leap from my seat, grab my jacket and truck keys, and… Fiddlesticks! I don't have a truck!

Really sorry for the last minute request, but any chance you're available to drive your Gramps over to City Hall?

I'll be right there!

I love that girl so much. Now I'll owe her another dinner. And I owe Scooby about a dozen makeup walks. I'm convinced he's well aware of this as he glares at me for walking out the door alone once again. "I'm so sorry, buddy; I swear I'll make it up to you," I reassure him, clicking the door shut.

Unfortunately, once again, my well-laid plans don't work out like I want them to when the receptionist at the main desk in City Hall tells me Councilman Whitfield isn't in and won't be back until after the holidays. Still, I take her up on her offer to leave him a message, but instead of handing it to her, I go down the hallway to Whitfield's office, where I slip the note under his door asking him to contact me. Then, just for good measure, I try his door, but of course, it's locked. It was worth a shot.

"Still won't tell me what you're looking for, Gramps?" Ellie asks when I return to the lobby.

"*I'm* not even 100% certain of what I'm looking for. I just have this nagging feeling I've missed something. Whatcha got there?" I ask her as she thumbs through a binder filled with laminated pages.

"Did you know they keep the records from the city council meetings in this binder for the public to read?"

"I did not. Should I have known that?" I ask, confused about what's in there that has her spellbound.

"It includes a record of who voted for what."

"Hmmm. That's nice." I still don't get it.

She rolls her eyes, before holding the binder up for me to see while she points to a specific line.

"Did you know that Councilman Whitfield voted to rescind the Pedals of Promise permit?"

"What? No. That can't be right. He's in charge of the Snowy Wishes Toy Drive thing. Why would he vote against *our* event?"

"It's right here," she insists.

I look carefully at the page. There it is in black and white. He voted yes. He was the fifth vote. The deciding vote. He could have voted the other way but didn't.

"Why would he do that? He seemed so friendly and helpful."

"He's a politician." Ellie shrugs.

"I guess. Still. That's disappointing."

I groan when my phone rings again, showing Greg's name on the screen. What now? How much bad news can a guy get in one afternoon?

"I have news," he says before I can even utter a greeting.

"Good or bad?"

"Hopefully good, but I don't want to get your hopes up because it isn't a sure thing, but *I'm* hopeful. And I don't usually say that."

Oh sure, the last time he called with that kind of news, it didn't turn out the way I hoped.

"Lay it on me," I respond after taking a deep breath.

"My office has been canvassing stores that were open all night when Ebenita was murdered."

"I see where you're going with this," I tell him, trying really hard not to get too hopeful. "Like convenience stores or gas stations."

"Exactly. But it's taken a while to connect with the people who were working that night."

My heart speeds up, but I remind myself not to fall for it this time. Not yet, anyway.

"We have a clerk who swears a man matching Sammy's description on a bike came into the store, drank Slurpees, and played pinball for two hours. Says he left a little before 1 a.m."

"Sammy loves pinball! Wait. Are you telling me the clerk says he was there at midnight?"

"Yes. *But.* And this is a very big but. I fear the prosecution could poke holes in this young man's story because he admitted he and his friends were smoking pot on the job."

"Okay."

"I've already requested a warrant for the video footage of that night, and it could take a while."

"Okay, let me know."

"What? What is it? Is everything okay?" Ellie asks nervously the moment I hang up.

"A gas station clerk claims that Sammy was there playing pinball at midnight the night Ebenita was murdered."

"Do they have video footage? Those places have cameras everywhere."

"They're working on it."

"That's it then! Sammy is free! Just in time for Christmas!" she squeals.

"We'll see. It never works that fast. And things have been moving extra slow lately anyway."

"I'm counting on a Christmas miracle," she insists.

"We'll see," I tell her. Don't get me wrong. If we have Sammy on video playing pinball at midnight, I will dance a jig in the middle of the street if they ask me to. Not that they would. That would be humiliating. But so far, nothing has gone like I wanted it to with this case, so I'll keep my emotions in check for the time being.

"I know what we can do!" she says.

"Let me guess. You want to go truck shopping."

"Unless you want me to chauffeur you for the rest of your life."

"No, thank you. I appreciate your taking me out today, but the sooner I can get back to driving myself, the better."

I nearly cause Ellie to crash as we drive along 28th Street toward the car dealership when I shout, "Wait! Stop!"

"What is it?" she says, swerving to correct her lane, earning her an angry honk and salty look from the driver next to us.

"I have to see that truck!" I exclaim, stabbing my finger against the passenger window for emphasis.

"The truck at the auto body shop?" she asks.

"Yes!"

"That doesn't really seem your style, Gramps."

"Just pull over!" I shout. "Please." I threw in the please for good measure when she glares at me for being such a pushy passenger.

"Ellie," I point at the dent in the right front fender. "This is the truck that hit me," I insist after finally convincing her to pull into the auto body repair parking lot.

"Are you sure?"

"Look!" I point again. "That's paint from my truck."

"Whoa. You're right. We have to find out who owns this!"

Ellie and I sprint toward the repair building when my phone rings *again*. I swear my phone has rung more today alone than it has in the last month.

"Mr. O'Sullivan, it's Mrs. Jensen," Irene tells me when I answer while continuing our dash to the building.

"Mrs. Jensen, I'm kind of busy right now. Can I call you right back?"

"Sure. But he might be gone by then. Or she. I can't tell for certain."

"Hang on a second," I tell her, stopping in my tracks, lifting a finger at Ellie to pause. "Gone? From where? And who are you talking about?"

"I'm sure someone is in Ebenita's house—at least their shadow. I'm looking at it right now. Lester says I'm out of my mind, and it's nothing but a shadow from a big plant, you know, just like with the clock thing where I got mixed up, but I'm certain someone is over there, and you said to call you—"

It always takes her a while to get to the point, but if she's right about this...

"Mrs. Jensen, lock your doors and stay in your house. I'm on my way."

"Ellie. We have to go to Ebenita's."

"Ebenita's? What on earth for?"

"Scratch that. You have to *drop me off* at Ebenita's and then drive straight to the police station."

"What's going on?" she asks, looking worried.

"Unless I'm mistaken, someone is breaking into a custom-made cabinet in Ebenita's house."

"Gramps! You need to call the police. You can't just go in there alone."

"There's no time. I have to catch the perp red-handed."

"Let me come with you," she begs.

"No. Do what I say. Please. I'll explain everything later. And feel free to speed. But only a little," I urge as she tears out of the parking lot. Where did she learn to drive like this?

Chapter 26

Ellie's car rounds the corner and disappears from view, leaving me alone on the sidewalk outside Ebenita's house. The eerie silence of the neighborhood settles over me like the calm before a storm. I make my way to the north side of Ebenita's, the side that faces the Jensen's, my steps careful and quiet. A mix of adrenaline and the weight of what I'm about to do tightens in my chest.

Peering through the side window, my breath fogs the glass, and at first, all I see is my own anxious reflection staring back at me. Then, as my eyes adjust to the dim light inside, a shadow moves across the room. Just like Irene said. My heart skips a beat, not out of fear but determination. Ebenita's killer is inside her house at this moment, and whoever it is won't get away like last time.

I make my way to the next window, crossing my fingers that somehow it's unlocked. Success! I gently ease it open wider and wider, hoping against hope it doesn't squeak. When I finally open it wide enough, I hoist myself onto the window sill, reminding myself once again that I'm no longer a young recruit fresh out of the police academy but a 67-year-old retiree who was recently in a car wreck instead.

With my feet firmly on the floor inside Ebenita's laundry room, I congratulate myself for pulling that off without making any noise. I slowly make my way to the living room, which is stark and unadorned. The bare walls are devoid of pictures, and there are only minimal decorations, including the ugliest statue I've ever seen. It's so ugly I'm momentarily distracted as I stare at it. I'm mesmerized by its enormous nose and ears and bright red shoes.

Then I see it. A large, antique cabinet sits against the wall where Councilman Marc Whitfield is opening it with the key he stole from me.

I curse softly when my next step lands on a creaky floorboard, forcing Whitfield to spin toward me. Before I can decide how to take him down, he slides a single-action revolver from his jacket pocket, and points it at me.

"You don't belong here, O'Sullivan," he growls.

"And you do?"

"Just turn around and leave right now. Forget you ever saw me."

"You know I can't do that," I tell him, my voice steady despite the pounding in my chest.

His gaze hardens. "Then I'll have to shoot you."

I swallow hard, the reality of the situation pressing in on me. "Tell me why you did it first. Why did you murder Ebenita?"

He pauses like he's contemplating whether he should tell me. But I must know. And maybe buy myself some time to think of a better plan.

"Ebenita was blackmailing me," he admits.

"How?"

"She found out I took bribes to advance some development projects in town. and I knew the evidence must be here somewhere, but I didn't think to check this antique cabinet when I was here last time. Who keeps blackmail evidence hidden in the middle of their living room anyway?" he scoffs, waving a stack of papers about.

"I guess Ebenita does," I muse. "Hidden in plain sight."

"You need to answer a question now," he insists.

"Okay."

"Where did you get the key? Was she blackmailing you too?"

I roll my eyes at him. I won't justify the second question with a response. "I found it on the ground where you callously left her body. She must have dropped it when you struggled." The look of shock on his face almost makes me laugh. "How did you end up at the Starlight Community Center at midnight?"

"Ebenita suggested it. She swore she'd bring the evidence. But she came empty-handed, of course. She had the nerve to demand I persuade the rest of the council to approve another new development on the south side of the city. That's when I knew it." He pauses dramatically, like he's waiting for me to sympathize with his dilemma.

"Knew what?" I ask.

"I knew I'd never be free of her. Not by playing her stupid games anyway. No matter how much I helped her get what she wanted, she would keep coming at me. It was a vicious cycle I felt helpless to escape." His story unfolds like a tragic play, with a beleaguered politician as the unwilling villain pushed to his limit.

"So then I lost it. I just lost it. I was so angry I shook her. We struggled, and the next thing I knew, my hands were around her throat. I didn't mean to kill her. I hadn't planned to kill her. But I couldn't stop myself. I couldn't see beyond the white-hot rage that consumed me. After that, I raced home, where I kept waiting for the police. I knew they'd search her house and find the blackmail evidence. But then I saw on the news that they had arrested someone else, and I was off the hook." He laughs. Yes. He actually laughed. Gun or not, I'm ready to jump this guy.

I'm so incensed. "I couldn't believe I got away with it. Until you and Jack showed up at my office, that is."

Thoughts of jumping him in the next second are pushed aside by my confusion.

"I'm not following," I tell him.

"That's when I knew you were on to me."

"I think you're confused." About more than one thing, that's for sure.

"I'm not confused. You guys suddenly appear at my office, and I'd never even met you. Am I supposed to believe that was just a coincidence?"

"I saw you on the news while I was eating lunch," I explain. "You were talking about the toy drive, and I thought maybe you'd help us with our event. You weren't even on my radar at that point."

"But you would have figured it out eventually. In fact, you *did* figure it out," he says.

I nod. "And you ran me off the road."

The flash of anger I see in his eyes at that moment confirms my worst fears. He's desperate, cornered.

"Is that what gave me away?" he asks.

"Not initially. The shoeprints you left in the snow at the scene were unique."

"Ah yes, my Velluto's. I paid $1800 for those," he says, unable to hide his smile at the memory of buying outrageously priced designer footwear.

"When I was in your office, your assistant picked up a file folder from the ground with dusty shoe prints on it. I saw the unique pattern on the folder, but it was so out of context and busy and noisy in your office that I didn't consciously connect it. Until today that is, when I reviewed the crime scene photos. That's when it started to come together. Then, when I learned you voted in favor of Ebenita's proposal to rescind our event permit, I realized it had to be more than just you being a two-faced politician."

"Huh. Okay, enough chit-chat," he declares abruptly. I have to dispose of you and these files, but I can't do both at once," he complains, waving the gun and the papers toward the couch. "Sit over there while I think."

I pretend to comply, but just as I start to walk past him, driven by a surge of adrenaline and determination, I pivot on my heel, lashing out with my fist in one swift, practiced movement, knocking the gun from his hand where we watch it fly across the room landing with a thud against the far wall.

Surprise flashes in his eyes before he moves to get the gun, but I still have the upper hand. I barrel into him, my shoulder connecting with his chest, sending us both staggering. The blackmail papers he had refused to drop earlier scatter like leaves in a storm, fluttering around the room in a chaotic dance. I like to think it looked like the final scene in the Christmas movie Die Hard when the bearer bonds rain down on the bystanders after the explosion, but I doubt it was that dramatic.

We careen into an end table, knocking over a lamp and that ugly dwarf statue. Sounds of the shattering lamp fill the air, like a soundtrack for our struggle. Whitfield tries to push me away; his face contorted in anger and desperation. He's strong. Stronger than I anticipated, and I'm still weaker than I'd like from the wreck, but the stakes are too high to give in now. We grapple, each trying to gain the upper hand, knocking into more furniture and knocking over a wingback chair causing me to stumble.

The moment I falter, Whitfield lands a solid punch to my gut, knocking the wind out of me and dazing me, forcing me to step backward, slipping on the papers. He uses the opportunity to gain control, his hands finding my throat much in the same way they found Ebenita's.

The pressure builds instantly, his fingers tightening with a desperate kind of strength. Panic flares within me, my breath coming in short, ragged gasps as I claw at his hands, trying to break his grip. The world blurs at the edges, my struggle becoming more frantic. But just as the darkness closes in around me, I hear a sickening thud, and Whitfield collapses on top of me like a bag of rocks.

"Took you long enough," I tell Detective Rodriguez, who's standing over us and glaring. The dwarf statue still gripped firmly in her hand.

Chapter 27

"Could you give me a hand here?" Dead weight is surprisingly heavy. Oops. Maybe I shouldn't say dead. He isn't dead, though. I hear him breathing.

Detective Rodriguez signals to the officers coming in the door to deal with Whitfield. They cuff him before rolling him off me, and from the noises he's making, I can tell he's coming around.

"Ellie must have found you," I tell her.

"Not quite."

"Is she okay?" I ask, worried something happened to her.

"She's fine. She should be here any minute now."

"So why the *not quite*?"

Detective Rodriguez paces around me like she's about to devour her prey.

"I admit, at first, I thought this key you were going on about might mean you hit your head harder than anyone realized. Even though the doctors said you were fine..."

She trails off to pause and glare at me some more before continuing. Uh oh.

"I mean, why would the great Detective O'Sullivan remove evidence from a crime scene and keep it a secret for so long?"

Gulp.

"He would know that's illegal..."

Two gulps.

"Luckily for Detective O'Sullivan, I decided to follow up on his story because if this key truly existed, it shouldn't just disappear on its own. So, I went back to the hospital to lean on a few orderlies, and sure enough, one of them said, and I quote, 'this dude gave me a $100 bill to search that guy's pockets.'"

"$100? That's it?" I protest.

"That's your takeaway?" she scolds.

I guess I deserve a lecture. I'm surprised it took this long.

"So what happened when you finally realized I was telling the truth? About the key going missing, anyway."

"That's when I knew you were in trouble. Then, on my way out the door to track you down, the precinct called to tell me your granddaughter was there looking for me. That's when I realized you were in *big* trouble. so I raced straight here. And the rest, as they say, is history."

"You'll learn the details once I give my official statement to the department, but Councilman Whitfield confessed to taking bribes - the evidence is scattered across the living room in case you were wondering - *and* to murdering Ebenita *and* to running me off the road, but if you need more evidence, you'll find a pair of outrageously priced designer shoes at his house with an unusual tread pattern which matches the shoe prints found at the crime scene."

"I look forward to reading that report," she says.

"Oh my gosh! Sammy! I almost forgot. He'll be out in time for Christmas," I tell her after she reaches out her hand to help me to my feet. "Although, I couldn't find a place for Pedals of Promise, and now it's really too late-- What?" I ask when I see the pained look on her face.

"Don't count on Sammy being home for Christmas."

"Oh. Let me guess. Because it's Christmas."

"I'd like to say I could pull some strings with the courts, but it wouldn't help anyway. Any judge authorized to sign the release papers is long gone until the 26th."

"I understand. Now I need to contact the families who were expecting a big Christmas party and a bike to tell them everything is off. If they still want a bike, they'll have to meet me at the warehouse. And I no longer have a truck to deliver bikes to those who can't make it there. What a mess." I bury my face in my hands.

"Gramps!" Ellie bursts through the door, flinging herself at me.

"We have to quit meeting like this," I joke as she nearly knocks me over with her enthusiastic greeting.

"Quit putting yourself in these situations, and we won't have to!" she lectures.

"You should listen to your granddaughter, O'Sullivan," Detective Rodriguez adds.

"Thank you for saving him!" Ellie exclaims, throwing her arms around Detective Rodriguez, who seems rather taken aback by the gesture.

"Yes, well, just doing my job," she mumbles, her cheeks turning pink.

"So, when does Sammy get out of jail?" Ellie asks as Detective Rodriguez scurries away. Sure. Leave me to deliver the bad news.

"I don't think we can get a judge to sign the release papers until the 26th."

"No! He can't spend Christmas in jail!" Ellie cries.

"That's just the way the system works sometimes, honey. It's out of my hands at this point. And it's out of Detective Rodriguez hands as well," I add when Ellie turns to ask her.

"Does that mean no Pedals of Promise, either?" she moans.

"I'm afraid not. We have nowhere to hold a gathering that big."

"This really blows," Ellie complains.

"I hear you. I'm afraid the best we can do is make the 26th a happy homecoming for Sammy, and hope that the donors who are involved with Pedals of Promise forgive us for bailing on them this year and agree to an even bigger and better event next year. A Christmas movie miracle just isn't in the cards for us."

Chapter 28

CHRISTMAS DAY

This is one of those days that, despite my believing Christmas miracles only happen in the movies, *I* end up believing in the magic of the season after all. Stepping out my front door after having ducked into the house to get a scarf, I'm enveloped in the buzz of activity taking over our block. Yes, believe it or not, the event is here. I mean, literally here. In my neighborhood. And not one person has complained about parking. Ebenita tried to stop the Pedals of Promise event from coming, but it came anyway.

Thanks to Detective Rodriguez and a few influential and sympathetic friends, we were able to transform the event into a block party, and from the looks of it, the entire community turned out to celebrate.

A local band even showed up unexpectedly and constructed a makeshift stage, so now their music fills the air, a lively mix of Christmas classics and upbeat tunes that make it impossible not to tap my feet.

Strings of colorful lights crisscross overhead, casting a warm glow on the faces below, while the scent of cinnamon and pine mingle with mouthwatering aromas of every variety of delicious food you can think of. Tables are laden with food donated from restaurants and grocery stores, allowing plenty for those who need it to take some home at the end. As if that weren't enough, neighbors from across Boulder also brought homemade treats and snacks, and there are hot drink stands scattered throughout.

The local hardware store donated dozens of heat lamps allowing us all to stay warm despite the light dusting of Christmas snow. The centerpiece of the event, a towering Christmas tree (I have no idea how it got here, and I probably don't want to know), stands at the end of the block, its lights twinkling like stars, even in the daylight, with piles of donated gifts for all surrounding it.

Scooby and I weave through the crowd, greeted by familiar faces and warm smiles. Ellie insisted I pull Scooby in the childhood wagon she found in the attic.

"So he doesn't get stepped on!" she insisted.

I told her it would be too ridiculous and there's no way Scooby or I would agree to it. And that's why I'm now pulling my dog (wearing his new Christmas coat) in a festively decorated wagon piled high with blankets to keep him warm. I'm not sure why I even bother arguing with that girl. She's a mix of her mother and grandmother, and I should probably just give up now.

Scooby, of course, is in his element, happily accepting all the head scritches and treats from partygoers. He must be wondering how he got lucky enough to play host to a party in his front yard.

After I pause to enjoy a cup of hot cocoa, generously topped with whipped cream and a sprinkle of cinnamon, I spot Detective Rodriguez laughing with a group of teenagers.

"Detective Rodriguez, you outdid yourself," I tell her when she turns around.

"I think we can drop the detective for the day, Howie. It's Christmas, after all."

"Okay, Laura, you outdid yourself."

"I had a lot of help," she argues.

"But we couldn't have gotten the proper clearance if it hadn't been for you."

"Thankfully, the block party didn't require a special permit. Just clearance from the police department to close the street for the day," she points out modestly.

She's being humble. After we cleared out the crime scene last night, she pulled me aside for what I assumed was the scolding of my life. Instead, she shocked me by asking if I minded if she 'made a few calls.' Those few calls turned into an all-nighter for both of us, and despite my still thinking we'd never make it in time, we did.

"When are the bikes due?" she asks.

"Any minute now," I tell her. "I'm just sorry Sammy isn't here to see this and pass out the bikes, but the important thing is he'll be out of prison tomorrow, and we'll celebrate with him then."

"Hey! Here they come!" Laura shouts so loud the kids all go crazy.

I think I'm more excited than the kids to see the box truck arrive. With Santa at the wheel...

Where did the Santa come from?

"Who did you get to play Santa at the last minute?" I turn to Laura, who's beaming from ear to ear. Why is she smiling like that? I spin around to get a second look. Is that? It is! "It's Sammy!" I exclaim. "How? What? I don't know what to say!"

"Turns out I did have a string to pull." She laughs.

"I'll never be able to thank you enough!" I insist.

She places a hand on my arm. "My brother and I were raised by a single mom who worked two jobs just to keep a roof over our heads. One year, during a particularly lean Christmas, she told us we could each ask for one small present. I desperately wanted a bike that year but didn't say anything to my mom because I didn't want her to feel bad.

"Instead, I took a bus to the mall to see Santa. I wasn't sure I believed in him, but I was desperate. I even wrote a letter in case he forgot my address. Christmas came, and we each got our little gifts. I got a doll and I loved her. Of course, I was disappointed about the bike. I didn't really think the Santa thing would work, yet I was still hoping.

"Then came the knock on our door. It was the local police department, which was never a good sign, especially in that neighborhood where we were always suspicious of the cops. But Santa was with them. They had a big bag of presents for my brother and me. And several grocery bags of food. And..." She takes a deep breath.

"They didn't." I smile.

"They did. There it was, in the back seat of the cop car. A shiny pink bike with a plastic basket and ribbons dangling from the handlebars. I rode and rode and rode it until the front wheel fell off many years later.

"It turns out the mall Santa worked with the police department to hand out presents to needy families. I swore right then and there when I grew up that I would either be Santa Claus or a cop.

"Which one did you pick?" I laugh.

"My friends insisted I had a better chance of becoming Santa than I did a cop. Hang on a second. Are you crying, Howie?"

"No," I sniffle, turning away. "It's hay fever."

"It's December."

"I have winter allergies."

"Merry Christmas, Howie," Laura says, throwing her arms around me.

"Merry Christmas, Laura," I tell her, trying not to get her coat sleeves wet.

Don't miss the next book in this series **Fireworks & Felons!**

More Books by B I Skinner

Ghostly Glenwood Mysteries Paranormal Cozy Mysteries

The Case of the Haunted Hotel

The Case of the Pilfering Poltergeist

The Case of the Poached Peridot

The Case of the Gym Ghost

The Peach Cobbler Caper

The Case of the Haunted Radio Station

Spooky Shanty Realty Mysteries

Afterlife in the Attic

The Lifeless Listing (coming in August)

Holiday Cozy Mysteries (non-paranormal)

Sleigh Bells & Sleuthing

Fireworks & Felons

Marcall's Breakfast Cafe Paranormal Cozy Mysteries

An Eggscellent Day for Murder

24 Carrot Caper

Daggers and Donuts

Cupcakes and Corpses

A Crime of Cranberry

Peppermints & Pandemonium

Star Spangled Homicide

Blood Curdling Ballots

Sign up for my email list here

https://mailchi.mp/9ebce0da866a/email-signup-list

Visit my website

biskinnerauthor.com

Follow me on Instagram **@bethiskinner** Facebook **@biskinnerauthor**